Highl

A Highland Chronicles Tale

Cathie Dunn

Praise for Highland Arms

"Cathie Dunn's *HIGHLAND ARMS* is a deliciously atmospheric Scottish love story, well-spun and charged with deeply-felt emotion. Cathie Dunn has a true gift for historical romance."
~ *Jane Holland, author*

"A compelling story teller... Maybe just maybe love will find you along the way and take you into a journey of romance with a smuggler ... I canna wait for more from Ms. Dunn."
~ *Romancing the Book*

Ocelot Press

Copyright © 2018 by Cathie Dunn
Fourth Edition, 2019
Cover Art: Soqoqo Design
Cover Images: VJ Dunraven Productions / Dudarev Mikhail

All rights reserved.

No part of this book may be used or reproduced in any manner whatsoever without written permission of the author except for brief quotations used for promotion or in reviews. This is a work of fiction. Names, characters, places, and incidents are used fictitiously. Any resemblance to actual persons living or dead, business establishments, events, or locales, is entirely coincidental.

To Laurence.
Always.

Acknowledgements

Highland Arms was the first novel I completed, and I was fortunate enough to secure a publishing contract with a well-known US-based romance publisher within a year. Even though the rights reverted back to me in 2014, I will always be grateful to The Wild Rose Press for giving me that opportunity.

I must thank my lovely critique partners for their input, in particular Cait O'Sullivan and Denice Kelly. Your constructive comments and relentless nit-picking (well-meant, of course!) helped shape the original manuscript into something enjoyable.

A big 'thank you' goes to my author friends at Ocelot Press, who have welcomed me with open arms into their clowder. I'm thrilled to be part of this new, exciting cooperative of highly talented writers.

Lastly, my thanks goes to my husband, Laurence. Being married to a writer who dreams of kilted Highlanders roaming the hills with brandished broadswords can't be easy...

About the Author

Cathie Dunn writes historical mystery romance. She has two novels and a novella published.

Cathie loves historical research, often delving into the depths of the many history books on her bookshelves. She also enjoys the beauty of dramatic countrysides. She has travelled widely across Scotland, England, Wales, France and Germany.

Cathie lives in France with her husband, a rescue dog and three cats. She is a member of the Romantic Novelists' Association, The Alliance of Independent Authors and the Historical Novel Society.

Find her at **www.cathiedunn.com**

Highland Arms

Chapter One

Scottish Highlands, Spring 1720

"Angus, do stop whining! It's entirely your fault we're here." Catriona MacKenzie turned to glare at her brother riding a few yards behind her.

"Well, it *is* hellish," he insisted, his expression sullen. "A huge inconvenience. The wind is chilling, and my clothes are soaked from constant drizzle. And never mind the midges. Wretched things," he added, slapping his wrist to rid himself of a biting menace. His gaze met hers in a bone-chilling stare. "And before you forget, dear sister, if *you* hadn't dallied with John that night, we wouldn't be here."

"You know I did not *dally* with John. He tried to—" Catriona turned away from him, fighting off the tears. It was pointless trying to reason with Angus. She let her gaze roam the mountainsides of Glencoe rising high on either side of her. The peaks were hidden from sight, shrouded in low cloud. A shiver of foreboding ran down her spine.

If only Angus had not told Father.

She stared ahead, at the broad back of Robbie MacKinnon, the gruff guide her father had hired to take her to her godmother, Lady Margaret Cameron Macdonald. He was clad in a thick plaid, a shabby kilt that had seen better days, and brogues with thick bag socks. Despite his advanced age —he must at least be as old as Father—he seemed completely unfazed by the icy gusts that tore at the shredded fabrics. A stench of stable wafted around him. Not surprising the midges avoided him.

The small group was on the move from daybreak to sunset, the pace relentless, ever since they left Edinburgh a week earlier. Grinding her teeth to stop them from chattering, Catriona pulled the fur-trimmed cloak tighter around her neck for a little extra warmth. She should be snug at home, not in this wilderness scratching her insect-ravaged skin.

The lack of hot water for a soothing bath grated on her, and she hated the plain travel dresses, in earthy brown tones, blending her into the countryside yet to awaken from its winter slumber.

She stifled a sob. Where she was going, nobody would glance twice at a girl looking disheveled and mud-stained. No person of worth ever ventured this far from the city.

Sent from her home in disgrace, through no fault of her own, she was now far away from the luxuries she was accustomed to. Far from the balls, the dancing, and the afternoon tea parties which were the latest pastime for those fortunate enough to afford the expensive new treat. Instead, she was heading to the Highlands—a remote, lawless country. A land of cattle thieves and smugglers, rebellions and murders. She shuddered as dread settled into her heart.

The wind pulled her shawl off her shoulders again. She wrapped it over her cloak and fastened it anew under her chin in a double knot. Tilting her face up, she looked straight ahead. Whatever awaited her at her godmother's house could not be any worse than the recent weeks.

"Please don't dawdle, Miss," MacKinnon shouted. "We've yet a way to go till the Drovers Inn and night is closin' in fast." He jerked his head toward the dark clouds that drifted lower into the valley.

Catriona winced as she pushed her mare forward. Her legs burned, pain soaring through her limbs. This was torture.

Blast John Henderson! Everything was his fault. She scowled, biting back the tears that welled up and swallowing the bile that rose in her throat at the memory of that evening over a fortnight ago.

"Come on!" Angus pulled the reins from her hand and spurred his mount forward, jerking her mare into a canter. As any protest was futile, she remained silent and willed herself to ignore the pain.

A gust of sleet hit her frozen cheeks, the icy wetness mingling with her tears. She wiped them away with the back of her gloved hand but all it did was spread the dampness even further. A thin layer of white settled on her clothes and horse's mane. As thick snowflakes began to swirl around them, Catriona pulled her hood further down to cover her face and lowered her head to focus on the path in front of her.

***

By the time they reached the Drovers Inn, the hour was late. MacKinnon threw the horses' reins to a lad who appeared from within the stables at their approach. Catriona nearly slid off her mare with tiredness, her limbs numb and stiff from the long, cold ride. MacKinnon caught her deftly and carried her inside. She leaned against this strong, old man for a moment, careless of how it might look. He was kind, and it felt good to be looked after. He shouted something to a burly man sitting on a wooden chair near the fire who vacated it quickly, but with a scowl. Then he settled her gently into it.

"Thank you, Mr MacKinnon." With shaky fingers she peeled off her gloves, ignoring the pain searing through her bones. Never had she ridden a horse for so long.

MacKinnon nodded and scanned the smoke-filled room. "I'll find the landlord for some food and a room for you, Miss." He strode past several tables to a door on the far side and went through.

Catriona leaned back, untied the shawl, and breathed in the pungent scent of peat, wood and smoke. Angus came to stand next to her, staring into the flames, not saying a word. As her limbs warmed, Catriona shed her cloak, uncomfortably aware of her plain travel dress. She tilted her head to gaze around.

The place was like most inns they had stayed en route, only larger. Rough wooden benches and tables filled the space, the floor rushes filthy with the mud from the brogues or bare feet of the travelers. Smoke from the tallow candles in their sconces stained the walls and ceiling, their acrid smell mingling with the scent of burning peat. She shuddered. Hopefully this was the last time they had to make do in such surroundings before they reached her godmother's house. Surely the manor was comfortable, cozy, and, most importantly, clean.

A group of drovers huddled together at a table by the door through which MacKinnon had disappeared. When several looked her way, she quickly turned her head back toward the fire. From the corner of her eye she saw a green onion bottle containing a dark liquid being handed round, as they refilled their cups. They were talking about her, she guessed, stealing curious—or worse, lustful—glances, but their language was foreign. Many times in the last few days she had heard the Gaelic being spoken. It was very much the language of this wild country. Her mother was a native speaker but her father forbade its use in his house.

The men were discussing her openly, no doubt, knowing full well she'd not understand a word. She watched them through her lashes, not wanting to be too conspicuous. They were dressed in filthy plaids and shirts, several with dirty bare feet she spotted under the benches, unwashed for God only knew how long. Most likely even He with all His knowledge had no idea when they last cleaned themselves. Their smell, close up, must be revolting. She wriggled her nose.

Her gaze scanned the rabble, until it fell on one man who lounged on a chair at the side of the table. Her eyes widened. Completely at ease, tanned calves stretched out from underneath his kilt, he exuded raw masculinity. His leather brogues were muddy but he appeared otherwise cleaner than his companions, and more, dare she think it, sophisticated? She drew in a quick breath.

Intrigued, any thought of detection forgotten, Catriona let her gaze drift over him, taking in his worn kilt and plaid. The light-brown linen shirt gaped open at the neck, revealing a soft sprinkling of hair on bronzed skin; his sleeves rolled up over strong, muscled arms. His bearings put him above the other men in status but his body proved him to be a man of the out-of-doors. To her surprise, his chin was not covered with an unkempt beard—like his companions' shaggy faces —but only bore a hint of stubble. Here was a man who shaved regularly.

Catriona's mind whirled as she let her gaze wander further across his ruggedly handsome features. His open face with strong cheekbones and wide-set eyes spoke of power, a forceful character. Dark blond hair, glowing in the light of the tallow candles, was tied back at the nape of his neck. Most certainly he was not a drover. But why was he sharing their whisky? He piqued her curiosity and, in the absence of any other form of entertainment in this bare inn, she found herself fascinated.

When he glanced up from his cup, their eyes met. They held for a moment that stretched like eternity. His, a vibrant green that sparkled across the smoky room, mocked her apparent interest. Caught in the act, she blushed and quickly busied herself adjusting the folds of her dress before extending her hands to the fire, thereby turning her back to the room. How obvious her scrutiny had been! Her cheeks flamed, and not just from the heat of the fire.

She had never stared at a man that way, not even the most handsome of gentlemen who had danced and flirted with her during her first Season. It must be her tiredness. Her blush deepened when loud laughter followed a string of words she was sure that man muttered in a soft low lilt. Oh no, now they were laughing at her.

Angus turned from the fire and glowered at the crowd. He must be aware something untoward happened. Red blotches covered his cheeks. She knew the signs. Her brother had a temper. It tended to flare up quickly.

"Mind your own business," Angus growled at the men. He looked around. "Where's that rotten guide?" MacKinnon still had not returned. Shifting from one leg to another, Angus stared again at the men, now talking more loudly. Her brother didn't need to understand their language—the tone was clear.

Catriona pulled her gaze away from him when one burly

drover approached, cup in hand, his features hidden behind a bushy black beard and straggly long hair. The voices subsided, as silence settled across the room. Catriona held her breath. The man said something to her brother in the Gaelic and held his cup out to him. Angus bristled, pushing his shoulders back. It was obvious he was out of his depth in this place.

"Leave us be," he ordered, his gaze darting to the door through which their guide disappeared. The drover took another step forward and pushed his cup under Angus' nose. Catriona watched her brother flinch and turn away in disgust. The man glowered and threw his cup with its amber contents into a corner beside the fire before he straightened to full height. She stood and reached for her brother's arm to placate him.

A deep male voice cut through the silence. "Seamus!" The blond man she had stared at so inappropriately pushed his way past the drovers who all rose, ready to support their insulted companion.

Her eyes widened as the men cleared a path without hesitation.

So the tall Highlander was their leader.

Awe mingled with trepidation. Her breath quickened. He walked to the drover facing Angus and dropped his hand on the man's shoulder, whispering a few words in their strange tongue. The drover glared at Angus, then nodded and returned to his seat without another word. He picked up the onion bottle and took a large draft before setting it back onto the table with a thud. His companions joined him, their voices muffled. The stranger had averted a fight.

"Apologies for the misunderstanding," he said in a soft, low Highland drawl, his gaze shifting speculatively between Angus and Catriona. "My friend Seamus here only bid you welcome."

"Yes, that famous Highland welcome." Angus snorted. "He threatened me. You make sure he doesn't come anywhere near me again, or I'll demand satisfaction."

A smirk played around the Highlander's mouth, hidden in

an instant. Catriona saw it and stifled a sudden desire to giggle. As if Angus was any match for this man. She gave in to the urge to let her gaze travel the length and breadth of his body. Again. He towered above them by more than a head. She was a tall girl, yet her eyes were only level with his chest where the linen shirt stretched over fine muscles. Her fingers itched to touch the silky hairs that covered the exposed V below his collarbone, to feel the strength of the muscles underneath. She shivered, and firmly linked her hands together, lest they develop a will of their own.

Pull yourself together, lass!

Angus was out of his mind to threaten a man like that. Her gaze finally met the stranger's, and he bowed to her with a wink, silently acknowledging her scrutiny for a second time.

"Rory Cameron, at your service, Mademoiselle. I hope you can forgive our blunt intrusion." To her horror, his gaze returned the favor, raking over her body hidden underneath the dowdy, mud-stained gown. Her cheeks burned in embarrassment at her plain and dirty attire. She wished she looked her best for this man. In desperation, her hand flew to her hair, and she tried in vain to push some escaped strands back into the knot at her neck.

His eyes lit up.

Angus grabbed Rory Cameron's arm. "Don't accost my sister! She's a lady, way above you in station."

Catriona's eyes widened. Fits of laughter welled up inside her. Suddenly, she was a lady, no longer the harlot who brought shame on the family; the fallen girl banished from home? It was too ridiculous. She burst into laughter.

"Forgive me, Angus." She covered her mouth with her hand. Her brother's face contorted with anger, his cheeks and forehead a bright red, a deep furrow between his brows. Now *she* had enflamed his anger.

"Leave us alone!" Angus demanded of the Highlander.

Rory Cameron grinned, his eyes glinting with wicked humor. Although he could not possibly know the reason for her untimely outburst, he must have guessed all was not as it seemed. He shook off Angus' arm with ease and, after a final glance at him with a raised brow, returned to his seat where he picked up his cup and toasted her.

"Failte gu'n Gaeltachd, mo chridhe. Welcome to the Highlands, my...*lady*." The drovers laughed raucously, raising their cups in mock salute.

Catriona blushed, an entirely new sensation coursing through her body, making her limbs tingle in the most pleasing way. She turned and sat, her hands once again reaching out to the fire. But all she saw in the flames was the emerald sparkle of Rory Cameron's eyes, an unholy promise mirrored in them. Nonsense, she admonished herself and shook her head. It was all in her imagination.

When a door creaked open, she turned to see their guide stroll over as if he had timed his arrival. Angus took a couple of steps toward him. "Have you found us rooms, MacKinnon?"

MacKinnon nodded. "Aye, sir. Miss Catriona will have her own chamber upstairs but I regret to tell you that you'll be sharin' the main sleepin' chamber with other guests." His gaze darted to the drovers. Was that a glint she spotted in his eye? Catriona was sure he exchanged a glance with Rory Cameron. How wicked!

Angus simply stared at him. "Are you out of your mind? I demand my own chamber."

"All full, sir. Even I'll have to sleep in the stables." The guide shrugged his shoulders. Catriona watched him closely. He appeared to enjoy this. How much of the fracas had he witnessed?

"I don't care if you sleep in the pigsty. I want my own chamber." Angus crossed the room in angry strides and grabbed the guide's shoulders. All eyes in the room were on him again. To Catriona, it seemed like a well-enacted play. They, including MacKinnon, were winding him up. The thought cheered her immensely. Angus never expected to accompany her all the way to Loch Linnhe. This fate was of his own making. She hid a smile behind her hand, knowing if he spotted it, his temper would soar again.

"I'm sorry, sir. This inn has no other vacant chambers.

Only one for the ladies. And Miss Catriona bein' the only lady guest, she'll have the chamber to herself." Demurely, MacKinnon shook his head. "But your dinner will be served in the small, private parlor next door. If you'd follow me, sir. Miss Catriona." He gestured toward the door.

Catriona jumped up and grabbed her cloak, shawl, and gloves, a low growl in her stomach reminding her she was famished. A good meal and quiet night's sleep in a chamber all to herself was bound to restore her spirit. And knowing Angus had to share a room with several smelly drovers gave her a great sense of satisfaction. She beamed at the guide as she followed her brother toward the door to the parlor. The guide winked at her. Oh, she might come to like the Highlands after all.

As she passed Rory Cameron, his hand stretched out as if by chance, warm fingers sliding down her arm, sending delicious shivers throughout her body. Their eyes met, his piercing hers as if he knew how his touch affected her. He smiled.

"Sweet dreams, my lady," he whispered, before withdrawing his hand to pick up his cup.

Chapter Two

Rory Cameron stretched after he bid the drovers goodnight, or rather good morning given the time of day, and emptied his cup with one gulp. The fire of the *uisge beatha* had long since evaporated, yet the smooth liquid running down his throat still warmed him. He needed all the warmth he could get. Crossing the pass before sunrise would be no easy feat. Yet it was the only way.

He withdrew several coins from the pouch tied to his belt and threw them on the table in payment for the drink consumed all night. Again, the drovers had pledged their support for the cause. They had managed to sell all the cattle, even those bulls they had lifted—or 'borrowed' as he called it —from the Duke of Argyll's estate to the south. He grinned at the memory of the money those bulls made him, even after he deducted the drovers' extortionate but well-earned share. Argyll, the Jacobites' most powerful enemy, raged, but Rory was certain no trace led back to him. He chuckled as he wrapped his plaid tight around him, and fastened it securely against the harsh winds outside.

The chilly breeze hit him when he opened the door to the yard. With a heavy sigh, he left the heat of the inn and headed for the stables. All was quiet around him apart from the odd howl of a lone wolf in the distance. At leisure, he saddled his horse and led it outside. To his relief, the skies had cleared. The soft rays of the early morning sun crept over the hilltops like fingers stretching out across the expanse. As he sat up, his gaze fell onto a small window under the gables. That window belonged to the ladies' chamber. He had enjoyed the cozy room on several occasions, in female company. A vision of the lady who presently occupied the chamber swam before his eyes.

Catriona.

Despite her dowdy exterior, Rory was in no doubt she was a lady. Her whole demeanor exuded breeding. Poor lass, to be burdened with such a pompous fool for a brother. But where were they headed? What was she doing out here? Next time he met Robbie, he'd find out.

As he left the yard, heading toward the steep incline to the pass, his mind strayed back to her curvy figure, her long legs hidden beneath the mud-stained skirt. She was unusually tall for a lady. Was that her problem? Together with her windswept black hair, and her large, amber eyes, she resembled a witch. A bewitching lass. Perhaps she was traveling to meet a future husband? His gut tightened at the thought. *A shame.*

He shook himself out of his reverie. She was a city lass. Her upper class accent gave her away. His anger broke through. She was someone who'd put her nose up at the Highland customs she was sure to encounter on her journey. Someone who would not, *could* not possibly understand. 'Twas best he forget her.

In grim resolve Rory spurred his horse into a canter.

***

By morning the cloud had lifted, leaving the towering hills glistening with snow and ice in the early morning sunshine. Catriona wiped the condensation from the mullioned windows and gazed out, awed despite herself by the sheer beauty of the landscape. Again, MacKinnon woke them early, keen to reach their destination before nightfall.

While she dressed, Catriona heard the drovers leave in a ruckus of voices. Her mind drifted to the night before and her brother's unfortunate confrontation with Rory Cameron. She went back to the window and scanned the yard. Several of the burly men from last night went on their way, but their leader was not in sight. Perhaps he was still inside? As her pulse quickened, she swiftly packed her necessities and headed down the stairs.

Sitting in the cozy parlor, a fire hissing in the narrow grate, Catriona took a spoonful of porridge, careful not to burn her tongue on the sticky mess. Only half-listening to Angus complaining he hardly slept all night, her gaze shot up at the mention of Rory Cameron.

"The stench emanating from them beggared belief. That leader of theirs, that Cameron, was nowhere to be seen or I'd have exchanged a few words with him." Angus emptied his cup of ale.

Catriona's mind raced. If the Highlander had not stayed, where had he gone in the middle of the night? Too wound up to eat, her stomach in knots, she set down her spoon and stared out of the window. Resting her chin on folded hands, she wondered why the man affected her so. The depth of her attraction to him terrified and thrilled her. He was different, simply oozing adventure and danger. You would not find a man like Rory Cameron in Edinburgh, and most likely she'd never see him again.

As they mounted their horses, MacKinnon explained their route. "We aren't goin' to follow the drovers trail across the pass. It's too strenuous for a lady." With a smile of encouragement, he gave Catriona's mare a slap on the flanks, sending the animal into a trot. She grabbed the reins, steering the horse toward the path, laughing at the guide's insolence. He quickly caught up with her, leaving Angus to scramble after them. "Instead we'll stay on this trail. It'll shorten the journey but this means we'll be crossin' the water."

She nodded. "Thank you, Mr MacKinnon. I wasn't looking forward to scaling those peaks." Her gaze scanned the shimmering surface high up, so glaringly white against the deep blue morning sky. Hidden under layers of cloud the day before, the steep hillsides now presented themselves in all their dangerous glory. Stunned by the beauty yet relieved she did not have to cross them, Catriona smiled as she gazed across crags as sharp as a dagger's edge.

Relaxing in the stillness of her surroundings, she was surprised at her own reaction. Instead of the misery that held her in its grasp for the last few weeks, a new sense flowed through her.

A feeling of...*belonging?*

She shook her head in disbelief. What brought this on? The eerie stillness should unnerve her, but instead it calmed and steadied her. Taking a deep breath, she gave her mare a nudge with her heel. Perhaps this journey was going to be good for her after all. No longer banishment, but rather an escape. Perhaps even a fortunate escape.

By the time they reached a small settlement by the shore of Loch Linnhe, the sun had crossed its zenith. Melted snow, and the footfalls of men and horses, turned the ground into a muddy slush. A handful of cottages stood scattered along the path, their walls covered in a thick layer of mud to repel the winds. Smoke swirled through holes in the roofs, filling the air with the smell of peat.

Catriona took a deep breath, enjoying the dusky scent. While she waited for MacKinnon to return from a cottage he'd entered on their arrival, she nudged her mare to the water's edge to let her drink. Her gaze roamed over the large loch, to the far shore and back to where a narrow arm of water branched off into Loch Leven, disappearing from sight between high peaks behind her. The rugged beauty pulled her in.

The guide came back a few minutes later. "The ferryman's out on the loch now. It'll be later today that we can cross over."

As he pointed to the corner of land on the other side, Catriona nodded. "Yes, I can see the ferry."

"I'm not going to cross the water in darkness," Angus barked. He tied his horse to a branch and came to a halt beside them. "Does nobody else own a boat?" He looked up and down the shore and pointed toward a row of boats bobbing in shallow water, tied securely to stakes. "Can't we use one of those?"

"They're fishing boats, sir," the guide said, a look of calm patience on his face. "And they need mendin'. Else they'd be out on the water too. Besides, darkness won't fall here as early as you're used to."

Angus' eyebrows shot together but MacKinnon turned to help Catriona off her mare.

"There ye go, lassie," he said quietly. "Take a stroll. We've got plenty of time."

She nodded and smiled. "Thanks for your help, Mr MacKinnon. We couldn't have done without you."

"Never mind, Miss. And it's *Robbie*." He inclined his head in an attempt to hide his reddening face and stalked away, her mare in tow, without another glance at Angus.

Catriona slid off her gloves, stretching her fingers, and tucked them into her sleeves. Crouching, she pushed her skirts behind her knees and dipped her hands into the icy water. The coolness chilled her but it also sent her pulse racing. This was refreshing. Bliss. A smile played on her lips.

"What's amusing you, sister?" Angus' voice invaded her happy thoughts. "Because I don't find our situation funny. No sign of an inn anywhere nearby, and we have to wait for the darned ferry boat to come in."

Straightening, she brushed her skirts down with wet hands and faced him. "Don't behave like a spoilt child, Angus, just because you can't drink yourself into a stupor." It felt good to see him flinch. Her remark hit home. "I'm going to sit on that felled tree trunk and take in the views. Do me a favor, find a seat somewhere else, and be quiet."

The incredulous look on his face lessened her shock at her own words. But so far away from home it didn't matter. It was her revenge for all the years of having to live with his lies, for being a silent, if reluctant, witness to his deceptions, powerless to end or reveal them to her parents.

Leaving him standing, Catriona marched over to the trunk, kicked it with her boot, found it solid, and lowered her bottom onto it. She wriggled into a comfortable position, spread her traveling skirts over her outstretched legs, and let her gaze drift over the water. A feeling of peace washed over her as her breathing deepened, drawing in the fresh air. She closed her eyes, allowing her senses to relax.

Later that afternoon they crossed the loch. The ferryboat

rocked fiercely with the waves. The horses were penned in, their scared whinnies mingling with the howling of the wind. Robbie stood at the helm, with the ferryman. Together, they stared ahead to the other side not saying a word. Highland men often kept silent, instead of wasting their breath, and time, with silly mutterings. Words of the kind her brother mumbled now. She rolled her eyes.

"I hate water." Draped over the side of the boat, his skin a pale-greenish hue, he choked. "I shouldn't have entered this hellhole. Should've just left you to it." He bent forward and retched into the water again.

Catriona smirked, having positioned herself upwind from him. It was not even worth pretending she did not enjoy his discomfort. Loudly, she drew in a deep breath of the cool sea air. "Father would not have allowed you to abandon me and you well know it. He may prefer you to me, as the son and heir, but I'm sure deep down he knows why you told him those lies." She grinned as she held a clean handkerchief out to him, and did not flinch when he slapped it from her hand into the choppy waves. "Suit yourself."

The outlines of the cottages on the shore ahead of them grew with each yard the boat shot forward. A narrow bell tower belonging to a small chapel stood by the side of the water. The low sun nudged the peaks on the far side, casting a warm, orange glow across the hills around her.

Admiring the surreal colors, excitement gripped her. Once they reached the shore, Robbie managed to calm the frightened horses and lead them back onto firm ground one at a time.

"It's only six miles to the manor, along the shore," he said, pointing to a narrow track veering off to the left. "Just behind that far bend." He helped Catriona mount her mare, and urged his horse into a trot, leading the way.

Riding in single file, Catriona and Angus followed him in silence. Eventually, their small party approached a large whitewashed stone house, a laird's manor, set halfway up a hill away from the water's edge. A path, just wide enough to allow two horses side by side, led to it. The brightness of the walls shone in stark contrast to the deepening evening glow.

Robbie steered his horse up the path. "Here we are, folks. *Taigh na Rhon*. The House of the Seal."

"Seal?" Catriona asked and turned in her saddle to stare into the shimmering water for a sign of the elusive animal. "Are there seals here?"

Robbie chuckled. "Och, aye. Plenty of them at certain times of the year. But that's not the reason for the name." He winked at her and touched his nose with his index finger. "Legend has it there's a beautiful cave nearby where the seals hide from hunters. Folks say a secret tunnel runs between the cave and the manor. Anyone wanderin' through that tunnel from the house will have to follow the cries of the seals to find the cave."

"Oh, how exciting! Perhaps I can visit it." Catriona clapped her hands together and laughed.

"Ah, lassie. Not sure if you can do that. You see, nobody in livin' memory knows where the tunnel is. Or the cave. Back in the olden days, half a century ago, smugglers used it all the time. Now, all that's left is the rumor."

Catriona's smile died as her anticipation evaporated. "Aww, what a shame. You think it was all invented? The tunnel doesn't exist at all?"

"Aye, folk have come to think so. But don't let me stop you tryin' to find it." He challenged her with a grin.

She laughed. "I'll have plenty of time to spare here, so maybe one day I'll go in search of it." Her gaze fell on her brother who cast his eyes toward the sky.

"Nonsense! Never heard such stupid tales." Angus shook his head. "You'd believe in faeries if someone told you they'd seen them."

"Not necessarily." Catriona retorted. "But the faeries might find *you*, dear brother. I'm certain Robbie has come across them out here. Haven't you, Robbie?" She winked at the old man.

"Aye. They love playin' pranks on fine city gentlemen."

"Oh, stop it." Angus pushed his horse past them.

The double doors swung open as they approached the

clearing in front of the house. An old woman wearing a plain linen dress, her graying hair tied into a tight knot at the back, came to greet them.

"So you have made it, my dears." She took another step forward and beamed. "You must be exhausted."

"Announce us to your lady, will you?" Angus bellowed, heaving himself from the saddle. "And call the stable boy."

The woman looked him up and down. Then her eyes, one brow raised in mock appraisal, met his. "I am Lady Margaret Cameron Macdonald, laddie, owner of this manor and the lands around it. You'll find the stables at the back. That way." She pointed to the side of the house, ignoring his flushed face. Turning her back to him, she opened her arms toward Catriona who was struggling to suppress the bubble welling up in her chest. A giggle burst through, quickly stifled as her hand covered her mouth.

"Failte gu Taigh na Rhon, Catriona." She pronounced her name in the soft lilt that reminded Catriona of the night before. "Welcome to my humble home."

"Thank you, Lady Margaret." Catriona stepped forward, awed and intrigued by the formidable Highland lady. Robbie took her reins and led their horses round the back, nodding a silent greeting.

"Go into the kitchen when you're finished with the horses, Robbie MacKinnon, and help yourself to some food and ale. And you, young lady, may call me Auntie Meg." She smiled, a warm gaze meeting Catriona's, and clasped her hands. "I am so proud to have you here. Follow me."

"Hey, what about *my* horse, MacKinnon?" Angus called after Robbie but the guide disappeared around the corner.

"You go and find the stables, Angus. Then you may join us in the drawing room." Auntie Meg pulled Catriona with her through the sturdy doors and pushed them shut.

Catriona giggled. "He won't like it. He's used to others obeying his orders."

"Well, lassie, he needs to learn that things are different out here. I take it he won't stay long?" Auntie Meg led the way along a barely lit, narrow corridor, past a huge oak cupboard that left little space for maneuvering.

Catriona shook her head. "Perhaps a day or two at the most. He hates the Highlands."

They came to a halt inside a small drawing room, comfortably furnished with armchairs and a settee. A fire burned brightly in a large iron grate. Auntie Meg turned to her.

"And you, Catriona? Do you hate it here, too?" She helped her out of the sodden coat and dropped it onto a chair. Catriona was too perplexed to protest. Auntie Meg was a lady. Did she not have any servants?

"It's beautiful. I..." She hesitated, not quite certain of her own feelings now that she had arrived. "It's quiet and peaceful. But so far away from home." Unable to hide the wistful note in her voice, she allowed Auntie Meg to nudge her toward a large sofa, covered with thick cushions.

"Fret not, lassie. It's never quiet for long. Nor peaceful." She nodded. "Now sit here by the fire and warm yourself up. I'll get the tea."

Only after Auntie Meg left her and she was lulled into a sense of contentment by the comforting heat, Catriona realized her godmother had called Robbie by his name. Did everyone in the Highlands know each other? A thought struck her. Would her godmother have heard of Rory Cameron? A delicious shiver ran down her spine.

***

After a brief chat with Auntie Meg over a cup of tea—real tea from the Colonies—Catriona retired to her room and slept for an hour. Although the fatigue from her journey still lingered, she felt refreshed, her mind settled.

She made her way to the dining parlor where the table was set, and a fire roared in a large stone fireplace built deep into the wall. Crossing the room, she went to the tall, narrow window and pulled the thick brocade curtains aside. With dusk settling, the view across the loch took her breath away. Low light shimmered on the water's surface, reflecting the last glimmer of the evening sky. Across the water, she watched the shadows sink deeper down the hills.

When the door behind her creaked, she jumped. Hastily, she dropped the curtains back into place and turned, expecting her brother. But it was not Angus who closed the door and faced her. Her pulse began to drum in her ears, and her hands shook from the unexpected surprise. She grabbed the curtains behind her for reassurance.

He leaned against the door, his dark blond hair washed and tied again at his neck. This time, his muscular frame was clad in worn trews and a fresh linen shirt, loosely fastened. A trace of mud clung to his black boots. She looked at his face and held her breath, caught as she was by a now familiar set of piercing green eyes. Her throat went dry. The last time she saw those eyes, at the Drovers Inn, they'd been friendly, even flirtatious. Now they were cold, dark, and as forbidding as a loch in winter, bereft of the warmth of the sun.

Rory Cameron.

Chapter Three

"What are *you* doing here?" Her voice croaked, and her clammy fingers fidgeted with the curtain tassels.

He remained silent, staring at her, the storm in his eyes relentless.

Her throat constricted in shock, she only managed a whisper. "I'm so sorry. How rude of me. I'm Catriona MacKenzie. From Edinburgh." Why was she so nervous? After all, this was not their first encounter. But who was Rory Cameron that he wandered freely around Auntie Meg's house?

As if he lived here.

"I know who you are. Now." The tone of his voice held none of the humor he'd shown at the inn, none of the flirtation. Instead, the chill in it sent icicles down her spine. His Highland lilt was strong, deliberately so, marking the difference to her accent. "Auntie Meg told me about you when she received your father's letter. Catriona, the fallen angel from the city." He snorted and let his gaze rake at will over her curves.

Heat shot into her cheeks, setting her skin on fire. What gave him the right?

"I'm sorry but you are misinformed." She crossed her arms under her breasts. The move did not escape his attention. He raised a fair eyebrow as his gaze focused on her décolleté. Quickly she lowered her arms again, entwining her fingers.

"Don't you worry, Miss MacKenzie." He laughed, though the humor never reached his eyes. "There won't be any temptation for you out here. Highlanders learnt a long time ago not to mess with Lowland ladies." He abruptly turned to the fire, grabbed a poker, and stoked the flames with fierce thrusts. The hissing of embers filled the room, and the rich scent of peat drifted to where she stood.

"Who are you?" Catriona stood rooted to the ground, her mind in turmoil. As far as she knew, her godmother had no close relatives, yet he called her Auntie Meg.

He put away the poker, and bowed to her in mock salute. "I'm Ruairidh Cameron. Just in case you've forgotten." He spoke his name with a Gaelic lilt, which he lost when he said: "Rory to those who don't have the Gaelic."

"I remember your name, Mr Cameron. You offered it at the inn last night." His eyebrow went up again. *Damn!* Why had she admitted it? She squared her shoulders and put her hands on her hips, her gaze meeting the challenge in his. After a long, silent battle, she blinked. "Are you related to Auntie Meg?"

A spark of surprise lit his eyes for an instance. Good. He should realize she was not a silly girl.

"Aye, my late stepmother was Auntie Meg's cousin. Distant relations, no blood ties, but out here family means everything, however far removed. Not like in the *city*." He spat the last word.

He must hate the Lowlanders. Catriona found that fact curious. "Well, you are wrong. City families stick together too." She raised her chin, daring him to contradict her.

He chuckled before settling into an armchair by the fire, stretching his long legs. A dark smile played on his lips. "Aye, that's why you're here, and not with your loving family."

Catriona balled her hands into fists. "You—"

The door opened and Auntie Meg poked her head in. Seeing both of them, she beamed. "Oh, you two have met already? Wonderful." She came over and hugged Catriona before leading her to a sofa opposite the armchair Rory Cameron chose. She pulled her down with her, leaning back into the soft cushions.

"I didn't expect you back so soon, Rory." She graced him with an indulgent smile. "This is perfect timing. I wanted to introduce you to Catriona personally but clearly you've acquainted yourselves already. I'm so glad to finally have my two dearest relatives with me."

Catriona watched in fascination. Auntie Meg must love him. Perhaps he worried her presence might endanger his inheritance. After all, Auntie Meg must be in her eighth decade, with a large estate to call her own, and no heirs.

Rory Cameron smiled at the old lady. "Yes, Miss MacKenzie and I have indeed met. Last night, in fact." His face transformed, the cold in his eyes replaced with deep affection. "And as you've asked, the last transaction was completed early, so I have a little time to spend at home."

This is his home? Dear Lord!

His words made Catriona feel like an intruder. Well, she *was* an intruder. Auntie Meg patted her hand as if she guessed her discomfort.

"That's wonderful, Rory. No doubt you'll have time then to show Catriona the estate. Perhaps you can even take the boat out onto the loch?" Auntie Meg beamed, not noticing the tentative look between her and Rory. "And you must call each other by your given names. No airs and graces here."

Rory's eyes bored into Catriona's. Contempt lurked in them, quickly replaced by something else. A challenge? Just what went on inside that man's head? Her mind whirled, sent into a dizzying spin by the intensity of their locked gaze.

They were saved from a reply when the door opened once again. Angus strolled in, his expression sullen as always. When he spotted Rory Cameron he stopped in his tracks. His frown deepened as his complexion darkened. "You?"

"Hello, Angus," Catriona said sweetly.

"Sister." He barely acknowledged her, and completely ignored Auntie Meg. Instead he stared at the man looking too much at ease in his chair by the fire, intentionally so, no doubt. "What are you doing here?" His hands clenched into fists by his side.

Rory Cameron looked at him with eyes the hue of slate. "As I told you last night, my name is Rory Cameron. I also happen to be a distant nephew of Auntie Meg's." His body appeared relaxed, yet his eyes were alert, his gaze not once leaving Angus' face.

Catriona realized Rory Cameron had not even attempted to use his Gaelic given name, nor spoken in the soft drawl he used earlier. His English now sounded *upper* class. This man was full of surprises.

"Angus, come sit with us." Auntie Meg rose and took his arm. He shrugged it off, ignoring the look of shock on her face and slumped onto the settee next to Catriona, taking Auntie Meg's space.

Catriona glared at him. Her brother seriously lacked good manners. This was the side of him their parents never saw, his true self. She shuddered. She was about to rise from her seat when Rory jumped up and offered Auntie Meg the armchair, which she gratefully accepted. Slowly, she let herself sink into its depth while Rory went to stand by the side of the fireplace, his quizzical gaze resting on Catriona. She inched away from her brother.

Angus stared at Rory Cameron. "You haven't answered my question. What are you doing here?" To Auntie Meg's affronted stance, he replied, his voice defensive, "We were assured this house was a safe haven for my sister. The presence of a strange man is quite unacceptable."

Meg Cameron Macdonald sat upright, eyes blazing. "Listen to me, laddie. I'm delighted to offer Catriona a home —something your father refuses to do. *You* didn't even help her when she needed a brother, yet you dare make assumptions on the virtue of *my* house?" She tapped her fingers on the mahogany arm of the chair. "Let me tell you one thing, Angus MacKenzie, I can assure you by the end of her stay, that is whenever your dear papa decides to have her back, Catriona will feel more at home here at *Taigh na Rhon* than she ever did in Edinburgh."

Angus laughed nervously, holding his hands up. "I do apologize, Aunt Margaret. I did not mean to insult your person or your home. I'm sure it's all, erm, in order." His hesitation said more than his words, yet he continued in a smooth voice. "But you must understand my concern."

He grabbed Catriona's hand. "My sister is young and impressionable. The presence in this house of a grown man, who shares the company of cattle thieves, as he did last night, might prove to be her undoing. A man has needs, and in the absence of any distraction out here, Catriona may lead herself into thinking she'd developed feelings for him. In her naivety she wouldn't know when to stop giving in to her passion. That's how she ended up entertaining her former betrothed—who was understandably horrified by her wanton behavior—that fateful night."

Catriona pulled her hand free from his grasp and slapped him. "How dare you! You make me sound like a brainless tart. You know exactly what John tried to do. Well, I'll tell you something, *brother*!" She stood facing him, her hands on her hips, while he held his reddening cheek. "The sooner I see the back of you the better. Because finally I can have a life. Something you've always done your utmost to ruin." She sat again, tilted her face toward him, and crossed her arms. In her haughtiest voice she demanded, "Now apologize to Auntie Meg. *Sincerely*."

Her brother's face turned scarlet and his hands shook. He balled them into fists again, as if poised to strike her.

From the corner of her eye she saw Rory Cameron take a step forward, positioning himself next to Auntie Meg. He put a hand on her godmother's shoulder. Catriona felt strangely comforted by the move.

Angus' gaze went from Catriona's to meet the old lady's icy stare. He swallowed. "I do apologize. I meant no insult to your person."

"Nor your house," Rory Cameron challenged him, eyebrow cocked, mocking. Angus scowled at him.

"Nor your house," he repeated and rose. "Now excuse me. I seem to have lost my appetite." He banged the door shut behind him.

Auntie Meg's labored breathing echoed across the room. Her brother's mindless words wounded her. Ashamed for being so closely related to him, she knelt by Auntie Meg's feet, taking a bony hand between hers. Her eyes met Rory's and a silent understanding passed between them. Whatever their differences, they would never allow the old lady to be hurt. She squeezed the cold fingers.

"I've heard you offer up quite a meal, Auntie Meg. Is that so?"

Auntie Meg's eyes began to sparkle. A slow smile spread across her wrinkled features. "Aye, and it must be nearly ready."

***

The house was still, and the first light filtered through the gaps in the shutters when Catriona woke the next morning. Her mind returned to the previous night. It had been a quiet affair. Despite all her attempts at cheering Auntie Meg up, Angus' callous remarks left her godmother in shock, her bubbly nature subdued. Neither was Rory Cameron in a mood for chat. Several times that evening she felt his gaze linger on her, any thoughts of his safely locked away behind those impenetrable eyes. Did he regret having her in the house? He might even convince Auntie Meg to send her back.

She could not allow that to happen. Not yet. One day, she had to return home—just not yet. Her father planned to find her a new suitor, someone willing to overlook her *indiscretion*. Pah!

Once he found such a paragon of society, he'd send for her. Most likely, the chosen suitor would be a rich man, but what else? Old, grizzled, and frail? Or young and arrogant, cast in the same mould as her brother? She liked neither option but then, it was not her decision to make. One thing was certain—love did not feature in her marriage contract.

What if her father let Angus have a say in it?

The notion froze her to the core, and she sat up. Despite her fondness of Edinburgh, and its array of entertainments, the longer she remained here in the Highlands the safer she was from such a fate. Perhaps she'd even be allowed to stay on as her godmother's companion? Growing old without having to wed anyone. Remain a spinster for the rest of her days. It was not the most appealing option, but preferable to whomever Father or Angus might choose. Yes, she'd just have to convince Auntie Meg—and Rory Cameron—that she simply had to stay.

Her mind made up, she rose and wrapped a thick blanket around her shoulders. As her bare feet touched the wooden floor, she hissed at the chill. With no maid to call upon, she left her room and went downstairs in search of the kitchen. The thought of a warming cup of tea raised her spirits. Then she'd continue to set her plan into motion.

She pushed the kitchen door open and stopped short. Standing by the mullioned window, in front of a large bowl overflowing with water, was Rory Cameron. He turned as he heard the door. Catriona caught her breath and grabbed the handle, letting go of the blanket.

Water dripped over his head and down his torso, trickling in small rivulets over his kilt held by a broad belt with a round silver buckle in a Pagan design of interlacing swirls. The light curls of hair on his tanned chest glistened with moisture. His shoulder-length hair was unbound, falling softly over taut muscle. A dry smile told her she was staring at him. *Again.*

She swallowed hard. "I..." She stuttered. "I'm so sorry, Mr Cameron." She averted her gaze to her feet. "I was just going to heat up water for my tea. I didn't mean to interrupt."

The insufferable man laughed as he grabbed a piece of cloth and began to pat himself dry. "I don't think you did." He shook his head, sending strands flying before rubbing it vigorously. "And it's Rory, remember?" He grinned. Catriona stood rooted to the spot. Words failed her. Her mouth went dry.

"But tell me," he went on, "do you always venture into the kitchen so early? If so, you'd better get dressed next time."

Transfixed by his mocking gaze, her cheeks heated as she became aware of her own state of undress. What an impression was she giving him, with her hair falling loosely over her shoulders, and the blanket only barely covering her modesty?

Oh, dear God, the blanket!

She pulled it back over her shoulders with shaking hands and wrapped it firmly around her. With a mumbled excuse, she turned and fled back upstairs into the safety of her bedroom. Still shaking too much to calm down, she slumped onto the edge of the bed.

Never had she seen her brother or father without proper attire, nor did John Henderson have much of a chance to remove his layers that fateful night—and now here, at the first glimpse of a bare male chest, she reacted like a silly maiden. She took a deep breath. My, he was magnificent. What would his chest feel like if she let her hands roam over it? Her fingers itched at the thought.

Catriona shook her head. What on earth was she thinking? With determination, she pushed Rory and his tempting body from her mind and began to dress. Not an easy feat with trembling hands.

A knock on the door startled her. Quickly, she slid into a gown and held it in place with her arms. "Who is it?"

The door opened a couple of inches. A young female face, covered in freckles, peered through the gap. "I'm Mairi, Miss. Lady Meg's maid." She hesitated. "I'm here to help you dress."

"Oh." Catriona sent a silent prayer of thanks Auntie Meg's way. The wilderness showed signs of civilization after all. She smiled and waved Mairi to enter. Today she'd look her best in weeks. The thought cheered her immensely.

***

Rory watched the door bang shut behind Catriona MacKenzie. Shaking his head, he dropped the cloth onto the shelf and slid into his shirt before draping his plaid over his shoulder. A plain silver clasp, swiftly attached, held it in place. He picked up his dirk, sheathed it at his belt, and glanced back at the door where only moments earlier this vision stood. Catriona.

Her thick black hair spread over her shoulders, framing her pale face, eyes wide in shock. A glimpse at her full cleavage, half-exposed by the blanket slipping from her grasp, left him with unholy thoughts of running his hands over her generous curves. Bare, pale toes peeked from underneath a thin, sheer nightgown, an item so out of place here; it made him want to rip it off her. Or was that just an excuse?

Mad! He shook his head and opened the door to the yard at the back. Carrying the bowl outside, he drained the dregs into the long grass. *I must be out of my mind. The girl is trouble.* He knew the moment he spotted her at the inn.

Oh, he had met her kind before. Edinburgh was full of them. Playing innocent while at the same time leading the most steadfast of Highlander to their downfall. No doubt, she'd start poking her nose into his life, and his activities. And she was bound to end up in Auntie Meg's will. No doubt about that either. Best for her to return to the city where she belonged. To play with some half-wit heir who would rush forward to wed her, compromised or not.

He must forget the vision of her slim thighs lurking underneath the fabric of that nightgown, her parted lips when she stared at him, her exposed, slender neck, the length of which his lips itched to explore inch by inch. Rory swore and dropped the trough with a bang. *Stop it!*

In the pantry, he ripped off a still warm chunk of bread, and cut himself a thick slice of cheese. Never do business on an empty stomach.

Then he set off.

Striding across the grass behind the manor, he took a bite as he mulled over his next move. He hoped that *dandy* Angus returned to Edinburgh soon. He could not risk any strangers to uncover his affairs. That included the lass. He'd have to make sure she stayed far away from his usual meeting places.

Rory stopped short. Yes, that was the idea. *Make her want to leave.* Then when she returned to her city, life would go on as before.

Moving on, he grunted at Auntie Meg's request to show

Catriona the estate. Aye, he'd show her the land, the loch, and the hardship of life out here. She'd soon be horrified at the dirt, the graft, and the unpredictable weather. He chewed on the last bit of cheese and wiped his hands on his kilt. No, he'd not let her endanger his plans. He knew ways of stopping her. At whatever cost.

As soon as he crossed the brow of the hill behind the manor, the building disappeared from sight. Rory took a sharp turn left and after another mile, climbed back down toward the shore, his brogues sliding on the mossy rocks. A short while later he reached the ramshackle boathouse where he kept his vessel. He pulled the narrow boat to the water's edge, but before leaving the shelter of the shed he scanned the shore.

Nobody in sight. Good.

Gliding out of his hiding place, he jumped in and pushed away from the beach with the oars. The manor was safely out of sight. The *dandy* was probably still asleep and if not, Rory was sure he'd not venture far from the house. As for the fine city lady, she probably suffered from an attack of the vapors after seeing him in the kitchen. He grinned.

Rory focused his mind on rowing. Deep breath and go. And again. Staying as close to the land as he dared, he took cover underneath the trees growing on the shoreline, their branches reaching far into the loch like long-fingered hands. He worked his muscles hard until he reached the small sandy inlet hiding the entrance to the cave.

When the boat scraped the ground, he jumped into the shallow water and pulled it up to hide under shrubs overhanging the rocks. He brushed away all traces of the vessel from the sand, and then walked to the rocks rising high against the bay, erasing his footprints behind him. Skirting around the promontory, he ducked underneath a large overhanging boulder that hid the entrance.

Rory waited inside until his eyes adjusted to the shadowy light, then groped behind a crevice for flint and a torch. Swiftly, he lit the torch and slid the flint back into its hiding place.

Only now was he able to see the path ahead of him. The tunnel was so narrow that a broad man like him barely managed to squeeze through, the exposed skin on his arms scraping the ragged stone walls. Only Rory and a small number of his associates knew of this passage.

Holding the torch in front of him, the flickering light illuminating the narrow shaft, he descended along the path. After a quarter mile of uneven ground, the path grew narrower, and lower. He crouched to avoid the sharp edges jutting from the ceiling. Rory was so familiar with the twists and turns he could walk it in his sleep, and it was not long until he arrived.

The end of the tunnel opened into a wide cave several times the size of Auntie Meg's parlor, with four openings in the walls leading to smaller chambers. Rory walked into each chamber and found them all empty, as expected. A fortnight earlier, the drovers collected the last few crates of the arms he'd hidden here following the previous year's aborted rebellion and taken them to a safer hiding place. All was going to plan. Soon, the Stuarts would ascend to the throne once more.

Chapter Four

Catriona decided to put the morning's shock firmly out of her mind. Now she took breakfast in her brother's company. The only sound that broke the silence was the spitting of the wood in the fireplace. Mairi informed them Auntie Meg felt faint and decided to remain abed. It pricked Catriona's conscience, and made her even more ashamed of her brother who shrugged the news off with a bored expression, not even bothering to look at the maid as he stared into his teacup.

Mairi's assistance in dressing her earlier that morning raised Catriona's spirits. She had washed off the remaining dust from the road and dressed her properly for the first time since her journey began. Mairi brushed her hair back in a loose plait, leaving a few stray curls to tickle her cheeks. Invigorated and refreshed, Catriona refused to allow Angus' sour demeanor to spoil her joy.

He stuffed his mouth with soft bread and cheese while she took her time. This was far better fare than the breakfast of boiled porridge they'd eaten whilst on the road, the taste of thick gruel still etched firmly into her tastebuds. In contrast, the bread was still warm, falling apart when she ripped off a chunk, a pleasure to relish.

She glanced at him across the table. Would it not be the crowning glory of the day if he returned home this very morning?

"When will you be leaving?" She prayed her voice sounded subtle.

Angus looked up, his mouth full. He chewed frantically, and washed the food down with a gulp of tea. Auntie Meg's China cup lay cradled in his long fingers. If he were to press them together ever so lightly, he'd crush the delicate cup like rose petals.

"I'll leave on the morrow. That Robbie MacKinnon apparently has some business to do here today. Not a clue what it is but hell, I'll be glad to see the back of this place." He poured himself more tea, ignoring her half-empty cup, and settled back, swirling the liquid in the small vessel. "It's depressing out here. Nothing going on. Dead."

"Perhaps that's a good thing," Catriona mused. "After all, I'm here to avoid temptation, remember?" Her gaze shot arrows at her brother. Why, oh why could he not leave today?

Angus laughed. "You'll probably end up fumbling in the hay with a crofter." Despite his outward humor, his voice was like ice. "Or that rogue from last night might have you for some bedsport."

Catriona's cheeks burned. In fury, she hoped, and not at her brother's lewd suggestion that she shared a heady bed of grass with Rory Cameron. The memory of Rory's bare chest, strong muscles rippling underneath dark skin, was almost too much to bear. Her color heightened further. Her brother must never guess. "He is Auntie Meg's nephew. And she told me he's hardly ever here." She took another bite of bread, trying to keep her features bland.

Angus' eyebrows shot up as his eyes searched her face. Dear God, was she so easy to read? A cruel smile sneaked across his clean-shaven visage. "So...my little sister finds the man appealing? Now that will be of interest to Father, I'm certain." He set the cup back onto its saucer and leaned forward to study her face. "Maybe I'm right after all, and you'll end up as his mistress. From what I saw at the inn, the man seemed to like rescuing damsels in distress."

"How dare you!" Catriona jumped up, reaching for the back of her chair just in time to keep it from crashing backwards. "You are despicable."

She stood behind the chair, clinging on to the solid wood. For strength, for support. To stop her from reaching out and punching her brother's arrogant face. Enough was enough.

"I know about the women, Angus. And about your debts." Angus stared at her, his features frozen into a grimace of anger. He pointed a finger at her but that did not stop

Catriona from saying what she needed to say. It was vital for her to get this out in the open. Too long had she suppressed her fury, her disappointment at her wastrel brother.

"I know about the Artisan Club. Yes, I even know the type of women you prefer for company. It's the buxom blondes, isn't it?" His eyes widened. She was right. "And to top it all off, I sent the debt collectors on their way. Repeatedly. Before Father found out. I promised them you'd pay them soon. And I nursed your valet back to health after those awful men beat him in your stead. Did you ever thank him for saving your neck? No, I thought not!"

Catriona took a deep breath, realizing she had raised her voice and the servants—or worse, Auntie Meg—might hear her. Quietly, she shook her head. "You're a big disappointment as a brother. All my life, I've taken it upon myself to make sure you didn't become that disappointment as a son to our parents. They deserve so much better. So, dear brother, who do you think is going to save them from finding out all these horrible things while I'm out here? Nobody! Now you're on your own."

He sat back in his chair, his face ashen. All anger seemed to have drained from him. Still he did not speak.

"You've done the worst thing possible for either of us, Angus, when you betrayed me. Even when you went downstairs on the night of the Spring Ball to tell Father, you knew John sought to ruin me in my bedroom—and that I was fighting him off. You thought you'd turn our parents against me. Instead, you got rid of the only person keeping you whiter than white in their eyes.

"I hope they find out for themselves what I've had to hide for so long. I'm sorry for the pain it will cause them but it's high time they knew. Whether you'll still be their golden boy after all has become public, I don't know." Her voice finally faltered. She had said her piece. Now she must move forward, without looking back.

Angus whistled sharply as he exhaled. "Have you quite finished yet?" He raised an eyebrow and waited for her to nod.

"There's nothing for them to find out, sister. I settled my financial affairs before we traveled, and I'll endeavor to avoid the Artisan Club in the future." He laughed, the sound harsh and bitter. "Even if I do end up in that place again—yes, I know I'm weak—our parents are never going to find out and you, my dear, will never breathe a word." His grin, devoid of any humor, made her skin crawl. "I have a plan."

Catriona shivered at the icy resolve in his voice.

"You see," he continued. "You may find yourself being married off to one of my associates on your return. I've already suggested a couple of names to Father. Either of the men are perfectly capable to deal with your forthright manner. They wouldn't mind whipping you into shape, and certainly wouldn't care if they're handling damaged goods as long as the price is right."

"I'm not damaged goods, Angus." Catriona's body trembled, her constricted throat choking her. "You know as well as I do that nothing untoward happened."

Tears welled at the memory. She had been so terrified when John Henderson, then her betrothed of six months, forced his way into her bedroom during the family's annual Spring Ball. Managing to fight him off with a candlestick, she'd been relieved for once to see her brother arrive at a timely moment. But instead of defending her he struck a bargain with John and went downstairs to tell Father. John escaped lightly and together the two despicable men ruined her reputation—even though her body remained intact. Hatred, deep and destructive, soared through her blood. She swore never to forgive Angus.

"Yes, but something might have happened if I hadn't come in, if John got his way. I know the kind. He'd have taken what he wanted, at whatever cost. And my two associates know just how to get what they want, as well."

She pulled herself to her full height, and looked down her nose at him. "You can't threaten me, Angus MacKenzie. Remember, I'm stuck in this wilderness until Father relents. So even with all your attempts at matchmaking, a decision might take a long time."

Angus chuckled. She bit back her tears, wiping the remnants from her eyes with the back of her hand. She didn't want to give him the satisfaction to watch her cry. Not any more.

"Father listens to me, don't forget. I'm a good son. Thanks to you covering my misdeeds he's none the wiser."

"He'll eventually hear about your transgressions. Like you said, you're weak and the gossips never stop. The truth will come out."

"You're so naive, little sister. The basic issue here is—I'm a man. So is Father. At the end of the day we're all the same, deep down. I'm certain he'd understand that I've got to go and enjoy myself while I'm young. But as regards you, my dear, I'm afraid the matter is quite the opposite.

"On my return home I'll introduce my friends to Father. He'd see it like this—they protect his good name, covering *your* dirty deeds by marrying you. Does that not sound like a fair deal?" He rose, winked at her, and walked to the door.

Catriona did not move, her nails digging into the back of the chair. Her face stung with anger, a fast pulse echoing in her ears. He'd still play with her life even when she was hundreds of miles away. She'd never be rid of him.

"You wouldn't do that, Angus. You'd get nothing out of it." She looked into his stony eyes, searching one last time for the link that made them brother and sister. She found none. His sardonic smile made her skin crawl.

"Oh yes, sister. Actually, I'm due to gain quite a lot. Father's inheritance. Control over *all* our family affairs. This includes yours through your future husband—a friend of mine who'll be only too delighted to share my indulgences. The cash I'll receive from the fortunate man in return for your hand. The manor in Edinburgh. The house in London. All that while I live my life as always, with the most pleasure and the least hassle. You'll have no choice but to obey. How terribly convenient." He grinned. "For me." The door slammed shut behind him.

Catriona stood, her body in tremors, bile rising in her throat. His threat was real. She had to do something to stop him. But, dear God, what?

She fled from the room and escaped through the front doors into the fresh Highland air. Lifting her skirts, she broke into a run. Breathing faster, she followed the path by the shore, escaping deeper into the wilderness. Gusts of wind tore at her gown, the skirts billowing in the strong breeze, then flapping flat against her legs again, almost bringing her to fall. Tears streamed down her face, but she did not wipe them away. She did not care. Blindly, Catriona ploughed forward, away from the house where Angus probably still laughed at her.

***

The sun stood still high in the sky when Rory returned. The meeting with his associates had been revealing. Robbie passed on vital information from the Lowlands that helped their cause enormously. His own clansmen brought news of the land. Support was growing. A few potential leaders lined up, provided Rory delivered the guns. Of course he could. He grinned. Hundreds of Spanish muskets lay hidden in the hills following that ill-fated rising the previous year. All those weapons were now at their disposal.

His small band of associates smuggled the crates out of the reach of the Royal Navy just in time. The Jacobites desperately needed them if they wanted their next uprising taken seriously. So far their boats avoided detection by government vessels—once or twice too narrowly for comfort. They'd eventually hidden their cargo in his cave for several weeks. Only recently had he given the order to move them further inland, with the help of the cattle drovers.

However as of late, the Navy had begun to snoop around on the loch as if following a tip-off. Was there a spy among them?

Everyone knew the risks. Brave men, committed to their cause, transferred the rest of the cargo to a safe, dry place deep in the mountains, where it remained until the time was ripe for another rebellion. *A successful rebellion.*

But the government patrols had become more frequent, both on land and on water, anticipating trouble from the Highlanders. A couple of weeks earlier, three men were caught with a dozen crates strapped to their packhorses. Rory went to Edinburgh, in his usual disguise as a merchant, looking for a way to rescue them. Instead, he'd watched them hang, their trial a speedy farce. All he could do was pray for their souls.

He clenched the oars at the thought of the torture, the pain they must have endured. Yet they never revealed any pertinent information. To him, they were heroes. He'd avenge those men. For now, the Jacobites were lying low, and biding their time. But they'd triumph in the end.

Rory steered back toward the boathouse. When he heard the crunch of gravel underneath the prow, he jumped into the knee-deep water, pulled the boat further inside, and tied it to a stake with a tight knot. As his eyes adjusted to the dim light, he spotted movement. In a swift move he drew his dagger from its sheath and turned. But what he'd thought to be a spy turned out to be a mermaid dressed in a deep blue gown.

Catriona.

Cursing under his breath, he approached her. She lay on her side, gown covered in sand and mud, her knees pulled up and cradled in her arms. The delicate lids of her eyes were puffy. Tears clung to her long lashes. She was sobbing in her sleep. What on earth had happened?

Rory sheathed his dagger and knelt by her side. Gently, he shook her shoulder. Catriona woke with a start and pushed herself into a sitting position.

"What…" She gasped, eyes wide in surprise. "What are you doing here?" Her gaze left his face to take in her surroundings. It came to rest where his hand still lay on her shoulder. He withdrew it and stood.

"I should ask you the same. This is *my* boathouse. And before you ask—yes, I do keep a boat here." Rory shook his head. She had invaded his privacy, yet made *him* feel like the intruder.

But it was obvious she was suffering. Her hair flowed down her back in thick black curls, the bows that had held it back caught loosely in the tresses. Mud clung to the side where she had lain. What had reduced her to such a state?

"Don't!" he said when she raised a hand from the muddy floor to wipe the tears from her face. "Let me." He pulled a scrap of linen from his sporran and knelt before her. "Don't worry. It's clean."

He smiled and took her hands when she tried to stop him, returning them to her lap. Carefully, he dabbed her soft cheeks and eyes before he crouched back on both legs, content with the result. Their eyes met, her long lashes framing the liquid golden depths.

What the hell happened to her? Did her dandy brother hurt her? Or was she crying because she missed the man she'd left behind in the city?

He rose, took her arm, and helped her up. "Come, I'll walk you to the water where you can clean your hands."

She stared at him in mute understanding, an assessing look on her face. He must ask Robbie about her background. The guide must have overheard something during their time on the road. Was she pining for the man who seduced her?

Rory led her toward the water's edge. She crouched on a boulder while he dunked the linen square, rinsed it, and held it out to her.

"Thank you," she said as she wiped her hands clean. "I must apologize. I think everything that has happened in the past few weeks finally caught up with me."

"No, Catriona. You don't have to apologize for anything." He took the linen from her, and rinsed it again watching the mud drain from it. Sitting beside her, he held out his hand. With apparent reluctance, she allowed him to push her mud-stained lace sleeves up to wipe the smudges of dirt from her soft skin. She shivered under his touch, a sensation that sent ripples of excitement through his body.

He felt the quickening beat of her pulse at her wrist. His loins contracted, and his own heartbeat rose to match hers. He released her arm and walked to the water. Dipping his hands into the fresh coolness, his breathing steadied. She was probably just chilled. After all, she should not have left the house without a cloak. Those fancy sleeves were for city summers, not the Highlands.

Rory turned to find her standing behind him. She stared out over the water, shielding her eyes with her hand against the glaring sun. Her lips parted as she breathed in the scent of the sea. The breeze from the loch played with her curls, sending them swirling around her head. She looked like a dark faerie, with her long tresses and golden eyes. Bewitching.

Dear Lord, what was he thinking?

"It's time we went back to the house, Catriona. You don't want to catch a cold."

She looked at him as if from afar. Then she nodded and turned toward the path. Rory unpinned the silver clasp that held his plaid in place.

"Wait." Coming to stand next to her, he wrapped the thick fabric around her shoulders, enveloping her into it with his arm. She shivered, again. Surely 'twas the cold. He tightened his grip around her and felt her sigh, and her body relaxing. Was she also drawing nearer to him? It seemed that way, as they set off at a stroll. His body hardened. But this time no cold water could douse the heat erupting inside him. He prayed she did not notice.

They headed toward the house. It was still out of sight but he spotted wisps of smoke in the air behind a small hill ahead. Good. She needed the warmth of a fire when they arrived home.

Her subdued silence unnerved him. "What happened?" he asked gently, keeping his gaze ahead.

Her body stiffened. "Nothing."

He pulled her closer against him, offering unspoken comfort. Though he towered a head over her, she fit snugly into the curve of his arm. Like she belonged. The heat inside him turned into a raging fire.

He glanced at her but she kept staring ahead. Increasing his steps, he hoped to douse the sensation with the cool air.

He had to put a stop to this now.

"So..." He purposely made his voice sound harsh. "You were hiding in the boathouse in a gown suitable for a soiree, crying your eyes out for no reason at all?"

"No. Yes." She took a deep breath and looked up, meeting his eyes. "My brother...insulted me. I will ignore him from now on."

Rory stopped and turned to face her, his fingers tracing the line of her chin, and her high cheekbones. Her eyelids fluttered yet she didn't shy away from him. Most interesting. He smiled and pulled her closer, the plaid enveloping them both in a warm embrace. Why not give into what his body told him to do? After all, she had freely submitted to a man's advances before. And while enjoying himself he'd also ensure she kept her freckled nose out of his business.

"Your brother is an idiot." He bent down and brushed her cheek with his lips. She trembled. Her hands lay flat against his chest. He gently bit her lower lip, as his fingers traced the line of her slender neck.

Catriona clung to him, wrapping her hands around his torso. Rory kissed her chin and slowly inched toward the tender spot behind her ear, nibbling the flushed skin. A moan escaped her lips.

Rory realized too late his own body had already betrayed him. His breathing was ragged—the pressure in his loins almost too painful to bear. He'd lost control. So much for using her to his advantage. He must never lose control again.

With more effort than he anticipated, he took a step back, holding her at arm's length. Her eyes fluttered open. Her cheeks, so pale not much earlier, turned crimson. Large amber pools stared at him as her hands withdrew from his back and flew to her mouth. A sense of loss coursed through him. Turning away, his arm and plaid still draped around her shoulders, he muttered, "We should be moving on."

Catriona shrugged his arm off. "Yes, we...we should," she stammered. "But not together." Her hands gathered her skirts as she pulled away from his arm and ran up the path toward the house, all propriety disregarded as she revealed shapely

42

ankles, her hair trailing behind her in the wind.

Rory stood still, deliberately taking deep breaths to steady himself. He watched until she disappeared around the bend. A spark had ignited between them, that much was certain. Slowly, he wrapped his plaid around him and secured the clasp back on his shoulder. Finding her in the boathouse was worrying. She clearly had a tendency to wander about on her own. The chance of her spotting him near the cave where he met his associates was too great. God only knew whom she might alert—inadvertently or not.

But it appeared he'd just discovered a way to distract her from poking her cute nose into his affairs. This could prove very useful. And once he'd had enough, he'd send her packing.

He simply must stay in control. He'd never give a stranger the chance to foil the Jacobites' plot. Their cause must prevail. The matter decided, Rory set off at a stroll back to the house.

Chapter Five

Oh Sweet Lord, she was cursed. Catriona slowed her step when she deemed herself safely out of Rory Cameron's sight. She was a sinner after all. A harlot. A strumpet. Angus was right. She was no different than the painted women who entertained her brother. She glanced behind her again but, thank God, Rory was nowhere to be seen.

Not wanting her aunt or brother to see her, she went around to the back of the house. Through the kitchen window, she spotted Mairi. With a shaky hand, she pushed the door open and entered. The maid turned to her and stared.

"What happened to you, Miss Catriona?" Mairi rushed forward but stopped short of touching her. "Were you attacked? We were worried about you, Lady Meg, and me. You were gone for so long."

"Just help me to my room, Mairi, to get rid of this mess." Her hands grabbed the folds of her dress, fresh tears burning in her eyes. "I just want to rest."

Mairi took her by the arm and led her up the stairs. Heat from the brazier kept her bedroom warm. The maid saw her glance over and said, "We thought you'd need to warm up after your walk. Little did we ken how much you'd need it. Here." She sat Catriona on the bed to remove her shoes, "I'll have water heated for a bath, Miss. We don't want you to catch a chill."

Catriona stood on bare feet, holding her arms up for Mairi to remove the sodden dress. She'd never wear it again. "I'd love a bath. But do stop calling me Miss. Out here, I'm plain Catriona."

Mairi laughed. She shook the dress out, leaving Catriona to fall back onto the bed in her shift and stays. "As you wish,

Miss. Though you're anything but plain."

She grinned as she dropped the dress beside a chest by the door and picked up a linen sheet kept near the brazier. Then she sat on the bed and set to work untangling the bindings of Catriona's stays. "You must've turned quite a few heads at those fine balls." She smiled, removed the stays, and wrapped her into the warm linen. Catriona curled up on her side. The maid dropped the stays onto the chest, picked up the gown, and went to the door where she turned.

"It'll take a wee while but I'll get your dress back to its former glory. Nae worry. You'll be able to sparkle in it soon again. The men won't be able to keep away." She winked and pulled the door shut behind her.

Catriona sighed. What was it about her and men? Mairi's words only brought back the memory of her shameful actions. How could she allow a stranger to touch her, to pull her as close as he had? Shivers trickled down her spine, and she wrapped the warm blanket tighter around her. His kiss felt so different from John's rushed fumbling, his forceful kisses, and wandering, kneading hands. Rory's hands had wandered, too, yet the sensations they caused were different.

All-consuming.

Her whole body reacted in a way she never expected or experienced before. He made her quiver under his touch, her skin tingling where his hands left a trail. His kisses set her on fire, her whole being shaking with...*desire?* Was she falling for him?

Her eyes flew open. *No.* She glared at the wall, cheeks flaming. She rested a cooling hand against her scorching skin. He must have felt it, her acquiescence at everything he did to her.

How utterly embarrassing! And in full public view. Never mind no-one appeared to be around in this deserted land. The thought of someone witnessing her shameful display made her gag. She swallowed hard.

What if Angus saw them? Oh, dear God, please no! He'd force her into marriage to one of his friends with ease. She was a strumpet. How could she face Angus now, after *this*?

Or ever speak to Rory again? Even Auntie Meg was bound to guess something was amiss, and that it was all her fault. At worst, the gentle lady would send her back in even greater disgrace. She closed her eyes and let the tears flow, shutting out the world around her.

When Catriona came downstairs, refreshed from her bath and a brief nap, she had her feelings under control again. She'd be polite to Rory, ignore her brother, and be most attentive to Auntie Meg.

To her surprise, she found the dining table laid with silver cutlery and delicate porcelain plates. She had never seen such intricate designs, not even at her parents' house. Lifting a plate with both hands, she gingerly turned it over, examining each fine stroke of paint. Expert craftsmanship, definitely not native. With great care she put the precious object back in its place. How could Auntie Meg afford such luxuries when she lived in the most remote wilderness?

When Mother wished to buy a fine set for dinner parties with important guests, Father refused her outright. It was too expensive. Yet here it was.

Not daring to touch one she looked at the wine glasses, admiring the vibrancy of colors brought to life by the flickering light of the candles. Hues of blue, green, and orange flashed in the delicate glass as she moved. She caught her breath. Almost like a rainbow. She shook her head, remembering the plain crockery and glass used the night before. Why tonight? She turned when the door opened and Auntie Meg walked in, leaning on a sturdy walking stick.

"There you are, my dear," Auntie Meg came over to her and kissed her on the cheek. Catriona helped her settle into her chair at the head of the table, and leaned the stick gently against the sideboard. "I've been remiss in my attention to you, Catriona. I must apologize."

Catriona sat at her aunt's left as on the night before. "No need to apologize, Auntie Meg. I hope you're well rested." She picked up a napkin and folded it into triangles, smaller and smaller. Fear of facing Rory, or worse, Angus, settled in the pit of her stomach.

"I am, thank you. So much so that I hope to go out of doors tomorrow, should the weather—and Rory—permit it. I'm in need of some fresh air. Resting is all good and fine, but nothing invigorates the body and heart more than the fresh Highland breeze. Will you accompany me?" Her gaze fell onto the napkin, which Catriona quickly unfolded and returned to its place.

"With pleasure." She beamed at her godmother as she flattened the napkin with her hands. "I can't wait to hear of the stories Mairi said you have to tell. I want to know all about the house, the family, and the land."

Auntie Meg smiled and patted her hand. "I canna wait either." Her speech slipped briefly into dialect. "There is so much to know, my dear. So much for you to learn before..." She hesitated, her gaze resting on Catriona's face.

"Before what?" Catriona was puzzled. What was going on?

The door opened, startling them both, and Angus came strolling in, his gaze drifting to Auntie Meg's hand on Catriona's. The old lady removed it and folded her hands in her lap.

"Good evening, ladies," he drawled and walked over to the cabinet where he poured himself a generous measure of whisky. "This is fine stuff, Auntie Meg. I'd take some to Edinburgh if you had a keg to spare." He came over and sat facing Catriona. "To your health!" He emptied the glass and set it on the table. Clearly, it was not his first drink of the day, and not likely his last.

The old lady bristled. "This is a fine *uisge beatha* from the glens in the north. It's not for sale or taking."

"And you've consumed enough of it anyway, brother," Catriona added. She turned to Auntie Meg. "Would you like me to pour you some wine?"

"Yes, dear, if you don't mind?"

"Not at all." Catriona rose and walked over to the sideboard to pick up a carafe filled with a glowing, ruby red liquid. She opened the stopper and breathed in the heady scent. It was high quality wine, most likely from Burgundy.

Again, she wondered how this remote house held so many alien luxuries. She had just poured a small measure into the Venetian glass at her aunt's side when Angus' hand shot forward, dangling his glass in front of her.

"I don't mind some either, sister." He grinned, his gaze challenging her to decline. Shrugging, she gave him what he wanted and filled her own glass last before placing the carafe on the table by her side, well out of her brother's reach.

Angus stared at the crystal glass in his hand, then his gaze wandered over the table, taking in the precious plates. "This is nice crockery. How the hell did you get it? Not even Father owns such exquisite items." He fingered his plate but stopped with a grin when a bony, wrinkled hand slapped his.

"Do tell me, Angus, dear. Were you born rude or did you turn into such an obnoxious character in one of your *gentlemen's* clubs?" Auntie Meg's eyes blazed.

Catriona opened her mouth to reprimand her brother when the door opened again. She glanced over as Rory entered, and caught her breath. She had not seen him since their encounter earlier in the day, and she was surely not prepared for this. He wore a white shirt with ruffles at neck and wrists, shiny black boots, and a pair of cream-colored breeches that clung tightly to his muscled legs. No plaid tonight. No kilt. No other adornments. Only his hair was tied back at the neck with a ribbon.

Rory's watchful eyes locked with hers for a moment. It seemed like an eternity. Shocked with her reaction, she lowered her gaze to her hands fidgeting with the napkin again. What was the matter? In the city, she had seen many gentlemen well-attired. But never before had the sight sent her heart racing, and her stomach aflutter. What made *this* man so different?

"Good evening, all." He strolled over, gave Auntie Meg a peck on the cheek, and took his seat opposite his aunt's. "May I?" He pointed at the carafe. Catriona held it out to him, their hands touching briefly as he took it from her, and she pulled hers back as if burned.

She felt rather than saw all eyes on her. Damn! As she

turned her head, she met Auntie Meg's gaze. Following an assessing look, a slow smile formed on the old lady's face. Catriona pretended not to notice and glanced at her brother.

Angus stared at her as if deep in thought. The corners of his mouth twitched, yet his was not a smile but a smirk. She did not dare look at Rory, but the memory of the passion she glimpsed in the depth of his eyes earlier came to her unbidden. His kisses that caused her legs to buckle, and aroused her nearly to the point of no return. She blushed. *'Twas a good thing he broke it off.*

Picking up her glass, she sipped at the wine. Too late did she realize it revealed her shaking hands.

Pull yourself together, Catriona.

Firmly, she set the glass down, her gaze melting into the colorful play of crystal and red liquid.

"So that's how the land lies." Angus exclaimed as he lifted his own glass, casting a knowing look between her and the Highlander. A darting glance revealed Rory's face, his expression inscrutable as his gaze in turn traveled from Angus to Catriona. When their eyes met, he cocked an eyebrow. She wanted to run away. Not since John's advances in her bedroom had she been so mortified.

Just as she decided to excuse herself on some spurious excuse, Mairi entered carrying a tray laden with delicate bowls of food. Grateful for the intervention, Catriona busied herself taking the bowls of steaming venison stew, carrots, and neeps, along with the loaf of freshly baked bread from the maid, and placing them at intervals on the table.

"Enjoy your meal." Mairi curtsied and darted out of the dining parlor. Catriona was not surprised. The tension inside was palpable enough to set the house on fire.

"Carrots, Auntie Meg?" She smiled sweetly.

They ate the meal accompanied by Auntie Meg's light chatter about housekeeping issues. Angus seemed absent minded, staring at each piece of crockery as if it was beaten gold, obviously assessing its value. Rory remained silent, only nodding his approval of his aunt's suggestions when prompted.

Catriona picked at her food, pretending to listen but not taking in anything. Her mind was reeling. Why must men all think the worst of her? Nothing was going on between her and that Highlander. Her fingers itched to slap her brother for his blatant insolence.

Only later, when Catriona retired to the drawing room with Auntie Meg, and settled over a glass of sweet dessert wine, did she find the courage to ask her godmother why she chose to use the nice crockery.

"Ah, yes. I thought we'd celebrate your arrival in our home properly, Catriona." The old lady gave her a warm smile before she turned impish. "And I wanted your brother to see that we're not just country bumpkins." She burst into an endearing giggle. "I think it worked."

Catriona stared at her. "You were winding him up? *On purpose?* Oh, you are wicked, Auntie Meg!" She laughed out loud and refilled her godmother's glass. "You definitely succeeded. His eyes nearly popped out when he saw the quality of your crystal."

"Aye, you could almost hear him do the sums in his head. He's so obvious, your brother. In fact, you don't seem like siblings at all, him so materialistic and superficial, and you so..." Her gaze lingered on Catriona's face. Heat rose in her cheeks under the old lady's scrutiny.

"So...?" she whispered, not daring to pick up her wine glass in case her trembling hands betrayed her again. Why was it she turned into such an emotional wreck after only two days in the Highlands?

"So guileless. So innocent," the old lady finally said. "You're also more sensitive. You hide your feelings, but not all too well."

"Hide my feelings?" Catriona asked, taking a gulp of her wine, its heady taste causing her head to spin. "I don't know what you mean." She looked up and met her godmother's gaze evenly.

"Oh, I think you do, dear. This whole episode in Edinburgh left its mark. And then here—"

"Edinburgh is history." Catriona's eyes blazed. "Father

chose to believe Angus even though he knows my brother lies through his teeth whenever he opens his mouth. Yet he still chose to believe the worst of me. How could he?" Tears welled up, unbidden and unwelcome, and she blinked hard.

Auntie Meg pulled a white, lace-edged handkerchief from a small purse at her waist and held it out to her. Catriona took it gratefully and dabbed her eyes.

"I'm sorry." She choked. "I didn't mean to interrupt you."

"Nae worries, dearie." Auntie Meg's voice was calm and quiet, soothing her frayed nerves. She patted Catriona's knee. "Your father is a creature of these uncertain times. He'd have lost face if he refused to punish you. It's always the women who have to pay. But I'm sure he'll call you back home soon, once the scavengers have discovered another scandal to gossip about. Fortunately, your engagement has been revoked. You'll be a free girl when you go back."

"You'd think that. But Angus has plans. Plans that involve his hawkish friends who are after girls with an inheritance. He wants to control my life. Use *me* to consolidate his business connections. And Father will probably believe it is for the best." She closed her eyes and drew in a deep breath. "I'll be a pawn in his games for the rest of my life." She sobbed and blew her nose, any pretence forgotten. She had no-one else to confide in, not even her mother.

"We'll see about that. Your life might change before he can set his plans into motion." Auntie Meg smiled.

"I'm afraid he'll be more determined than ever, after seeing how affluent you are. He'll expect me to inherit some of your wealth although I most certainly don't want to. His mind is always on money, and how to get more of it to waste on his pleasures." She dried her tears with the handkerchief. "I'm so ashamed he's my brother. And I know I shouldn't be. We are family after all."

"Aye, dear. Family is all good and well but where are they when you need them?" The old lady sighed.

"It's all my fault. If I hadn't left the salon, John wouldn't have followed me."

"That's nonsense. And well you should know it. The only

one at fault is John Henderson." She picked up the carafe and filled their glasses to the brim. "This is going to be a long night, Catriona. I want to hear all about that fateful incident. *And* about your brother and his associates. Then we'll decide what to do about it." She wrapped her arm around Catriona's shoulders. "Don't worry, lass." She raised her glass with her free hand. "Here's to your new family. *Slainte mhath*!"

Catriona pushed the handkerchief into her sleeve and picked up her wine, her mouth curving into a smile. "To your good health, too, Auntie Meg. And thank you." She took a couple of sips, savoring the rich flavor.

Catriona never told anyone about the taunts she suffered from her brother when she grew up. Nor had she ever spoken about her mother's obsession with appearances, which began when she was forced to relinquish her Highland heritage following her marriage.

It felt good to tell all, to share the burden. Her initial reluctance evaporated when she realized that Auntie Meg was genuinely concerned, and interested. They talked into the wee, small hours of the next morning, long after the house fell silent.

Neither Rory nor Angus disturbed them. Catriona wondered briefly whether they'd gone their different ways after the ladies left the dining parlor, or if they'd shared a drink. She did not think the latter very likely.

Much later, Auntie Meg yawned and glanced at the grandfather clock in the corner. It was nearing one of the clock.

"I'm glad we talked, Catriona, and I'm honored you confided in me." The old lady patted her hand. "No worries, dearie. We'll make sure your brother doesn't get his wish this time."

"But how? I'm at Father's beck and call. And Angus will direct him."

"Well, we won't give him a chance." Her small mouth was set in a determined line. "I shall retire now. When I rise your brother will hopefully have left us. And then we can focus on your future, lass." She rested her gaze on Catriona, a little smile playing around the lined edges of her mouth. She pushed herself from the sofa. Catriona jumped up and took her godmother's arm while the old lady clung to her walking stick with the other.

"I'll take you to your room, Auntie Meg, and then I'll come back and extinguish the candles. Leave it all to me." Affection filled her as she held the door open. They climbed the staircase slowly, Auntie Meg clinging to her arm. She was exhausted and Catriona felt a stab of guilt at keeping her up too long. "You'll have a long, undisturbed morning, Auntie. I'm sorry I kept you awake to such a late hour."

They stopped on the threshold to her godmother's bedroom. Embers of a fire still glowed in the grate, and a lit candle flickered on the little round table by the side of the oversized, ornate bed. "I don't want to hear any apologies," the Highland lady whispered. "It's been most enlightening. Good night, dear. *Oidhche mhath.*"

"Good night, Auntie Meg." Catriona kissed her godmother's cheek and closed the door behind her. On tiptoes, she hurried downstairs and returned to the drawing room to extinguish the candles and secure the brazier. Content all was safe, she tiptoed back toward the stairs, a solitary candle in her hand to light the way.

Her foot barely touched the first step when a grating sound came from the library further down the corridor. Aware the household was asleep, this could only mean one thing. An intruder!

She heard tales about the dangers of life in the Highlands. Unsure of what to do, she blew out her candle and left it on the bottom step. Best she remained unseen. The sound was repeated, though more slowly this time. She frowned. Surely the windows did not make such a sound. Steadying herself with her hand on the wall, she crept toward the door of the library. A faint glimmer of light illuminated the edge of the door. Relieved, she found it ajar, and nudged it open a little more.

A candle sputtered in a holder on the large desk. A shadow, the shape of a man, moved across her vision. She pushed the door open another inch. Then the shadow disappeared into the opening of the large fireplace.

Catriona blinked.

What?

She held her breath, her gaze steady on the stone frame. The shadow reappeared. He'd indeed walked through the wall. No other explanation made sense. It was a ghost. A tall, male ghost. She swallowed hard, and her trembling hands grabbed hold of the doorframe. Ghosts and ghouls were said to haunt old manor houses up and down the land. But never had she expected to see one of them.

Chapter Six

The candle was lifted, and Catriona flinched as it made its way to the door, a shadow looming large behind it. Her heart burst with fear, and her pulse pounded in her ears. She was certain the sound reverberated throughout the house. With her hands, she felt her way toward a tall store cupboard further along the corridor and slipped behind the far side, praying the ghost didn't come her way.

She made it just in time. Though the light of the candle illuminated part of the hallway her hiding place remained in the dark. She poked her nose around the edge of the cupboard and stared, nearly choking. The shadow stopped in the library doorway. She held her breath, trembling, yet unable to tear her gaze from the apparition. Did ghosts sense human company? What if it came her way?

And why did it need a light?

As the ghost raised the candle high, it illuminated hitherto hidden features. One glance, and she turned with a gasp, ducking back behind the cupboard, knuckles in her mouth as her teeth came down hard. Not a ghost, but a man. What was *he* doing here in the middle of the night, walking through stone walls?

But Rory's stern features were unmistakable. She sent a silent prayer heaven-ward, hoping he had not heard her. Catriona did not dare move or breathe. Then the light moved away from her, toward the stairs. As the length of the corridor was plunged into shadow, she peeked out to watch him hesitate at the bottom step.

Had he spotted her candle? But he moved on, climbing the stairs as stealthily as a cat in the night until he was out of earshot, and out of sight. Something in his manner told her this was a regular occurrence.

Catriona relaxed, taking deep breaths. After what seemed like an eternity, she crept forward, lifted her candle from the step, and very slowly made her way to her bedroom in complete darkness. Once inside, she turned the heavy lock, cringing at the noise it made, hoping fervently it had not alerted him. But his room was on the floor above. She should be safe.

Catriona dropped the unlit candle on the table by her bed, and by the light of the dying embers in the grate she undressed with still shaking hands. So, *Taigh na Rhon* didn't have ghosts after all, just Rory walking through the fireplace walls. The monstrosity was certainly large enough for a person to pass through. The frame was old-fashioned, at the height of a man's head. But Rory's height exceeded normal. However large the gap, he'd still have to crouch. But why sneak into the house in the dead of night through a hidden door?

Intrigued by his secretive behavior, she saw only one option—to take a closer look in daylight.

Catriona slid into bed, arranging the blankets around her. Clearly, he did not want anyone in the house knowing about it. She could not stop thinking about where the path led and what Rory was doing out so late at night? The whole mystery piqued her curiosity. As did Auntie Meg's unspoken plan. She snuggled into the warmth of the covers and pillows. The days ahead suddenly seemed less boring. Relaxing in the cozy wrap, she drifted off to sleep.

***

The dining parlor was empty when Catriona walked in the next morning, but she was unsure whether her brother had left or not. Knowing him, most likely he was still abed. Excitement gripped her the moment she awoke at an hour her mother called ungodly, despite her late night. She walked over to the sideboard and helped herself to a cup of tea. Earlier, she had gone to the kitchen — this time dressed —

and left her wishes for breakfast. Fresh bread and eggs.

Holding her cup in her hand, she sat with her back to the window to wait for her food. Once she was done, she'd go to the library. Best have a quick peek while the house was still. She jumped when the door opened. Grabbing hold of her teacup with both hands, she carefully set it down and glared at Rory. Damn!

"Good morning, Catriona," he murmured and raised an eyebrow as he glanced at the spilt tea on her saucer. "I didn't startle you, did I?" He strolled over to the sideboard and helped himself to tea. "Up so early?" he asked, his sarcasm obvious, when she remained silent.

Fuming, she forced a smile. "Yes, I just couldn't sleep any longer. It's a fine day, so I thought I'd make the most of it." Gingerly, she picked up her teacup again and sipped, holding her hand underneath it to stop the spilt tea trickling onto her dress.

Rory's gaze rested on the window, his eyebrow still raised.

He chuckled. "I guess you're talking about your brother's departure and not the weather?"

Catriona turned to look outside for the first time that morning. Usually the view stretched to the other side of the loch, outlining the hills in the distance. But today low, white fog hung over the water, obscuring it all. The mist reflected on the water made it seem much lighter. *Oh, a fine day indeed. If you loved fog.*

She turned back, her cheeks flaming, glowering at him. "Yes, of course I mean my brother's departure. What else would I mean?" She put the cup down and clutched her hands in her lap to prevent him from seeing her distress.

"So, where is he?" He took another sip, his gaze never leaving her face.

"He must still be asleep. He's a late riser." Why was she making excuses for her brother? This was ridiculous. Rory made her uncomfortable, his open scrutiny causing her to feel giddy like a little girl. He was a distant cousin, nothing more. She swallowed and met his gaze. "He has a long journey ahead of him."

"Aye, I believe so. Still, you'd think he'd rise early to get home quicker. Oh well, none of my business." He stood and put his cup back onto the sideboard. Stopping at the door, he turned and looked at her. "Sadly, as you can see, today is not ideal for sight-seeing, so I bid you good day." He winked at her and left her to her own thoughts.

Dear God, how infuriating he was. She slammed her flat hand on the table when Mairi came in bearing a tray of freshly baked bread and two eggs.

"Something amiss, Miss Catriona?" The maid went to the sideboard and picked up the pot of tea. Refilling Catriona's cup, she regarded her thoughtfully.

"Sorry, Mairi, 'tis nothing." She stared at her food, all appetite gone. Then she met the maid's gaze and squeezed her hand. "Thank you for this. It looks delicious. And do not fret, Mairi. Like I said, nothing's amiss."

"I saw Master Rory leave the room. He did not upset you?" The maid hovered over her, seemingly reluctant to leave her alone.

"No, Mairi. He did not upset me. Has my brother risen yet?" She broke off a small chunk of bread.

"Yes, but only recently. He rang the bell a little while ago for his morning tea. He's still waiting," she added, a glint in her eye. "Your breakfast was ready first."

Catriona threw her head back and laughed. "Well, best not keep him waiting too long, else he'll be stranded here for another day." She chuckled as she took a bite.

Mairi smiled. "Yes, Miss Catriona. I'll see to his convenience. And not to worry—all his bags are packed. Once he's broken his fast, he'll be on his way. Robbie is already saddling up." After a brief curtsey she left the room.

Catriona was still smiling when her brother walked in. She had just finished her breakfast, and was keen to make her move. The library beckoned. She sighed.

"Good morning, Angus." She put her plate and cup onto the tray and turned to him. "Are you ready to take your leave?"

"I'm sure this *is* a good morning for you." His face bore

no trace of a smile. The grim set of his mouth and the dark shadows around his eyes told her he'd been drinking more whisky the night before. "Yes, I'll be on my way very soon. But not before talking to you. Sit."

She bristled. "Sorry, I was just about to head out to—"

"That can wait. Sit!" He took her by the shoulder and forced her back onto her chair. She pushed against him but he held her down, showing a strength she found surprising. "Stay! I'm not going to tell you again."

She shrugged his hands off and leaned back. "What do you want to talk about, *brother*?" The chill in her voice surely made her feelings clear.

"You, my dear. Remember what I told you yesterday?"

Her eyes widened. What was he scheming now? "Yes, you mentioned some *gentleman* friends of yours." She nearly spat the word.

He chuckled. "I'm glad you remember. I did some more thinking on this last night and came to quite like the idea of you marrying a particularly trusted friend of mine. You see," he added, sitting opposite her, "I'd really like to help him. And you."

Catriona snorted, most unladylike. He was unbelievable. "You want to help me? How so?"

"You see, this gentleman comes from good stock, despite his...erm...indiscretions." He grinned at her, not a trace of humor in his eyes. "I'm sure I can convince Father to call you back home, say, in a month's time. By then a suitor will have come forward to rescue you from future embarrassments. That suitor will be Francis Moore. I'm sure Father will be happy to accept. It would take you off his hands, albeit at a good price."

Catriona shuddered. Francis Moore's reputation as a hell-raising rake was all the talk about town. True, he was of rich Lowland stock. But he was also a libertine. No lady of good standing would ever consider marrying him. The thought of letting him anywhere near her was repulsive. John Henderson had been a bad choice as a betrothed, but Francis Moore was far worse. She shook her head.

"I'm not a prize mare sold at market, Angus. How dare you! No way on earth would I ever agree to marry that...rake. I'll refuse to return if Father should agree to your little scheme. Now if you'll excuse me, I need some fresh air. Have a safe journey." She stood and marched to the door. He jumped up, his hand reaching for her arm which he grabbed in a firm grip, nearly twisting her flesh. She winced. "Let go! You're hurting me."

His face came close to hers, nose to nose. His eyes were dark, the look sending chills down her spine. He was mad.

"Listen, dear sister. You'll do as I say. You *will* marry Francis, and disappear out of my sight. You will attend the occasional ball with him, once or twice a year, and then leave him to his own life pretty much as he leads it now. And of course you'll bear him an heir. With his money, you'll want for nothing. Is that clear?"

She gasped, both at the pain and the audacity. The thought of such a marriage sickened her to the core. She knew the man in question, of his adventures, his pleasure-seeking lifestyle, and his abuse of girls young enough to be called children. Locking eyes with her brothers, she was in no doubt Angus was going to get his way. He'd convince Father it was for the best. For *her* best.

Catriona muttered through clenched teeth, "Go to hell. I'd rather stay here than return to do your bidding."

He suddenly let go of her hand, pushing her away. She staggered backwards, her hands seeking the sturdy edge of the dining table. It was all that kept her from collapsing.

"You'll do as I, or as Father tells you to, Catriona." He snorted. "Don't imagine for one moment you have any say in this. Unless, of course, you would agree to re-instate your betrothal to John Henderson. I'm certain John would be amenable to the suggestion—he appears to have taken a fancy to you for some inexplicable reason. Either way, your fate is sealed, sister, and I'm the one sealing it. A good day to you." He gave her a mock bow and slammed the door behind him. Sobbing, she collapsed into a heap.

Would she ever be free of him?

***

Rory pushed the oars with a determined stroke. He decided to go out on the boat, and not use the tunnel in the house, despite the thick fog hovering over the loch. He'd no choice unless he wanted to walk into the library and disappear in front of Catriona's eyes. Impossible!

He was sure it was her who hovered in the corridor the night before. The dandy would have made too much noise after all the whisky he'd consumed. Rory wrinkled his nose in disgust. The man was a wastrel. Good riddance to him.

But neither was it Auntie Meg or any of the servants. They knew not to roam around the house in the dark. But why did Catriona lurk in the shadows in the middle of the night when she should have been in her bed, fast asleep?

A picture of Catriona in her bed, dressed in the flimsy nightgown she had worn the previous morning, formed in his mind. Slim, white calves peeking out from under the thin fabric of the gown. Her creamy shoulders and the full shape of her breasts barely concealed until she wrapped the woollen shawl around her. His heart throbbed and his loins stirred with desire. It was months since he had lain with a woman. Of course he'd respond to Catriona's tempting body. It was not *her*, just bodily needs. Nature demanding release.

He remembered the day he parted with Sheonagh, his mistress of three years. She had been pressing him for marriage, nay, nagging him, threatening to become with child. He had long ago decided he was not the marrying kind. He had no desire for the responsibilities of fatherhood and family. These were perilous times, and he did not want to be bound to a wife and children. They represented danger, a trap his enemies could set to catch him in.

No, family life was not for him. He'd flirt with Catriona if he deemed it necessary, especially after her discovery the previous night, but all he really needed was a new mistress. As the memory of Catriona's curves invaded his thoughts again, he decided the sooner he found himself a wench the better.

Rory gritted his teeth and pulled harder at the oars. The fog would shield him from any prying eyes, English or Scot. And his mission kept his mind from encroaching thoughts of female temptation.

Rory capped his speed when he spotted the outline of the overhanging boulder. He turned to make sure his aim was correct, and that no-one wandered the shore, barely visible in the mist. Finding Catriona in his boathouse shocked him. But this entrance was too far for her to stumble across. And her dimwit of a brother should be gone by now.

Rory let out a slow breath as he eased the boat into the hidden inlet. As he neared the tunnel, he saw a torch lit just inside the entrance to the cave. Ah, he was not alone. Feeling the reassurance of his pistol and dirk, Rory lit his own flame and made his way through to the cave. More torches, flickering brightly in their sconces, lit his way. But, inside, he found no-one. The main cave was empty.

Rory wondered for a moment why his business partners left without extinguishing everything. Had they been in a rush? An icy shiver ran down his back. Had someone betrayed them? But the muskets were gone, so nothing of value could be traced back to them. He gazed into one of the smaller caves, holding his torch high up, illuminating the room.

Empty.

A groan made him turn quickly. He pulled his dirk and held the flame toward the far corner. "Who is this?" he bellowed.

"Mmhhh mmmhhhh," came the desperate reply.

Rory crouched in front of an overhanging rock and shone his torch into the darkness underneath. A pair of terror-filled eyes stared at him. A gag was stuffed into the man's mouth, and his arms appeared to be tied behind him. His legs were bound too, at the knees and ankles. Rory swore, shoved the dirk between his teeth, and grabbed the man by the shirt. With care not to bruise him, he heaved him out.

Then he stood back and looked his intruder up and down. It was nobody he knew, a young man, no older than ten and eight, bright red hair ruffled and muddied. He crouched in front of him, and, knife in hand, bent forward. He heard a sharp intake of breath, and the lad's eyes widened in terror. Damn!

"No worries, lad. I won't kill you." Rory cut through the gag, and the lad took deep gulps of breath. "Not yet anyway." He helped the captive into a sitting position and stood back, settling the torch into one of the empty sconces on the wall. The shadowy light flickered across the room.

"Who are you?" Rory held the knife casually in his hand, his attention not leaving the boy for one moment. Was he a spy, sent by the English and bound by one of his associates? Or a thief, bent on betraying them? If that was the case then his life was forfeit already.

"I'm..." the voice croaked. "Water. Need water."

Rory undid the flask at his hip and held it to the boy's lips, making sure his dirk stayed well out of reach.

"Drink slowly," he ordered. The lad did as he was told before shaking his head, indicating he'd had enough. Rory stoppered the flask and hooked it back into place, his gaze never once leaving the lad. This boy was no spy. He was too green behind his ears to make any attempts at freedom. "Now, who are you?"

"Jamie MacKinnon. Robbie's ma father. He sent me here to work wi' ye." The lad's face turned puce, an image that mirrored his father's. "I didna expect to be taken prisoner by tha' old man."

The indignation in the boy's voice made Rory burst out laughing. "What? Auld Cameron trussed you up like that?" He threw his head back and roared. "And you...a young laddie." Rory sat next to the boy and wiped his eyes. "Auld Cameron's in his 70th year, lad. You've a lot to learn." His shoulders were still shaking as he cut through the ropes.

"Thank you, sir." Jamie rubbed his sore wrists and ankles. Rory examined them, cursing to himself. Auld Cameron had done a safe job but the force he had used surprised Rory. The lad could not have untied himself even though it was in jest. Hence the burning torches, a sign that someone was here. But the lad could have died had he not come round when he did. Rory must have a word with his associate.

"Now, Jamie lad, I'll leave you here till your blood flows through your legs again. I'll just be in the next cave. Take things slowly. You get up too early, and you'll collapse like a newborn pony."

He shook his head and walked away. There was much work to do but it was too early for the lad to get involved in serious transactions. Robbie had spoken to him about sending his youngest to help. Little did he expect him to receive a welcome like that. Damn Auld Cameron!

He heard sounds of shuffling, and a thump. Ah, the lad had tried to stand. And failed. Rory shook his head and went over to where a narrow split appeared in the wall. He put his hand through it at head level, withdrew a scroll from the hidden compartment behind, and began unrolling it. He settled himself onto a ledge that served as a bench and began to read. After the first sentence, he swore. This was bad, very bad. He clenched his fist and slammed it on his thigh. The day started badly with Catriona spying on him in the wee small hours, and had gradually gotten worse. Now this beat it all. His group of men was infiltrated. He had suspected for some time but now he had no choice—he must confront Auld Cameron before he had the chance to reveal the muskets' hiding place. And move the arms again.

Chapter Seven

Catriona slid into the library and locked the door behind her. Earlier, Mairi told her Auntie Meg intended to rest until the afternoon, so she returned to her bedroom after her brother's departure for a bit of rest herself. Relief flooded through her as she lay on the bed biding her time.

She reconfirmed her decision. Never would she return to Edinburgh. If Father wrote, she'd ask Auntie Meg to allow her to stay. Beg on her knees, or do any work the old lady might ask of her—companion, housekeeper, anything. She doubted her godmother would send her back anyway. A smile brushed her lips at the memory of their late night chat. They had found common ground and forged a close bond. No, she was never going back. This was home now.

That matter decided, she turned her thoughts to another issue that intrigued her—Rory's strange night-time appearance in the library. Praying for patience, she waited for the staff to settle into their chores—and her chance to explore the fireplace.

***

Finally, she was in the library. While waiting for the house to quiet, she'd fallen asleep, only to awake an hour later, hoping she'd not ruined her chance.

Now, her back against the library door, she scanned the tall shelves stacked with innumerable books of all sizes and ages. Her mouth gaped as she stared at the array of literature—just how did Auntie Meg afford them? Remembering the delicate China, and the crystal wine glasses, Catriona wondered if perhaps Rory's middle of the night secrets had anything to do with it.

Her gaze moved from the shelves, across the comfortable leather armchairs, to the broad oak desk that stood in the middle of the room. Catriona strolled over and ran her hand across its grooved surface. Her fingertips slid over traces of wax splattered on one side, which most likely came from the candle Rory lit the previous night. Clearly, he'd not even attempted to hide any signs. He felt safe. The corners of her mouth twitched before she burst into a giggle, quickly stifled with her hand. 'Twas just her nerves. She'd soon find out what he was up to. A shiver of foreboding crawled down her spine, but she ignored it.

Gloomy shafts of daylight filtered through the narrow windows. Turning toward the fireplace, Catriona gazed at the dry logs piled in the center of the iron grate. Dust rose from the top log when she blew on it. Ha! Clearly, no-one had lit a fire here in a long time. Underneath the overhanging stone lintel, pitch darkness greeted her. She grabbed a candle from a holder on the wall and rummaged through the desk until she found flint and stone in a drawer. Quickly, she lit the candle and ducked underneath the lintel.

Straightening to full height inside the fireplace, she gazed upwards, holding the candle aloft, where blackened walls rose high up. The chimney must run the full height of the house, narrowing significantly toward the top. Only a dim, faint sliver of light showed its exit.

Catriona moved the flame along the crevices on the right hand side. There must be a switch, something to open the secret door. Her free hand moved across the stones, prodding, scratching, and pushing. But no magic opening showed itself. No uneven stone or ledge. She sighed as she stared at her hand, blackened with soot.

Standing still, she let her gaze move across the walls when her left cheek began to tingle. She moved the flame toward that side. It flickered. A draught. A draught meant a gap. She slid her hand over the crevices on the wall and cold air brushed her fingers. Yes, this must be the entrance. No doubt. The stone slab in front of her was large enough to climb through, the edges smooth from frequent use. Her heart pounded in her ears. The hand holding the candle began to shake. She grabbed it with her other hand and swallowed hard. *Focus*!

Containing her excitement, she pushed against the stone. It moved not an inch. She dug her fingers into the gap above it. Was she supposed to pull? But her nails slid off the surface and she stumbled backwards, hitting the back of her head. "Ouch!"

The pain stung, bringing tears to her eyes. She raised her hand to the wound but stopped short. The impact had felt more like a sharp object, not the broad stone of the narrowing chimney wall around her. As realization hit her, she turned and stared. A short metal knob stuck out from inside the lintel, level with her head, invisible to anyone lighting a fire.

But standing inside the fireplace it was quite obvious. If you knew where to look, that was. She smiled triumphantly and pushed it. Still nothing moved. Frustrated, she grabbed it and pulled. A scrunching sound made her jump, and she barely avoided hitting her head again. Catriona watched in wonder as the large stone slab finally slid from its place, leaving a dark opening.

A tunnel.

She'd found the tunnel. Dizziness nearly overcame her, and she toiled to steady her breathing.

Robbie's tale is true.

If the tunnel existed, then so did the cave. And the seal. She almost bounced with joy, but where she stood was no space for air jumps. Holding the candle in front of her, she peered into the darkness. The small flame barely reached beyond the entrance.

Should she go on, or wait? Perhaps tonight was better? But Rory might use it then. No, she'd go now and return before he realized she'd discovered his secret. Catriona lifted her skirt with her free hand and stepped over the threshold. Holding the candle aloft, she saw the large stone had moved smoothly into a narrow gap in the wall, pulled by some weird mechanism. Ingenious.

Her gaze scanned the surface for a lever. Yes! A metal switch, its surface shiny from regular use, protruded from the wall to her left. Her hand hovered over it, ready to shut the stone door behind her when she remembered she'd most likely return this way. What if it didn't work and she ended up stuck in the darkness, without anyone knowing where she was? No, she'd leave it open.

Taking a deep breath, she shuffled along the narrow corridor. It sloped downwards, and she held her hand against the wall to steady herself. She wandered on seemingly for miles, but it could only have been a few hundred yards. A draft came through from somewhere and while the air smelled a little stale, it had at least enough oxygen to stop her from feeling faint.

The absolute darkness around her began to play havoc with her mind. Distant noises made her jump. Something whizzed past her on the floor. Good heavens, a rat? Fighting nausea, she blinked hard. How far did she have to go? How far had she come? All sense of time and distance disappeared and she stopped. An eerie sensation took hold of her, as if someone was watching her. But only darkness greeted her when she glanced over her shoulder.

"Nonsense," she said out loud, her voice not quite as confident as she'd have liked. "No-one else is about." She'd have seen a torch, or some form of light. No-one could move quietly in this darkness, on uneven ground, with rocks sticking out all over the place. A tall, broad man like Rory would easily fill the whole space.

How did he manage? He must have been using this path for years. Years? A tunnel most likely leading to a cave, all hidden from prying eyes? Realization dawned on her.

No! It can't be true.

Shocked at the obvious proof of her earlier suspicions, she shook her head. Rory a smuggler? *Nonsense*! Smugglers were ugly brutes—criminals.

But then, what did she really know about him? Auntie Meg had said very little, only that she trusted him with her life. Catriona took a tentative step forward, her mind reeling, her ragged breaths breaking through the silence. The tea, the fine dishes and glass, the ferociously strong *uisge beatha*.

Rory Cameron was a smuggler.

And Auntie Meg must be aware of it, possibly even covering his tracks. Oh, dear God, she'd walked from one trap right into another. Life here was not safe either.

Shaken to the core, she steadied herself with one hand on the wall, the other clutching the spluttering candle. Her feet hurt from the sharp rocks, and she felt dirty and disheveled, with layers of dust covering every inch of her. Ever since entering the tunnel, Catriona pushed several cobwebs from her face, but the thought of spiders crawling in her hair made her wobble. She shuffled ahead, tears stinging her eyes.

What on earth was she doing? She was alone. Her family didn't want her, and here—where only this morning she thought she'd found her safe haven—she'd found a nest of criminals.

She sniffed and wiped her eyes with the back of her hand. Staring ahead, she blinked. The light of her torch showed two paths veering off. To her left, the tunnel continued downwards, widening, its ground well-trodden. The other fork was darker, and narrower.

With a firm nod to herself for courage, she followed the path to the right for several twists until she finally saw a faint, flickering light in the distance. Not far to go. Surely that was the famous cave of the seal? Anticipation mingled with dread and her pulse began to race. What would she find?

With tentative steps, keeping close to the wall, she approached the light. A secret opening, hidden from sight. While this must mean safety for a man fleeing from the cave, it did not afford Catriona a clear view. Voices reached her. Instinctively, she stayed out of sight of anyone on the other side of the stone wall. It might not be Rory. Straining her neck, she tried to listen to the words.

Just at that moment, a loud bang reverberated through the gap and along the tunnel. She jumped, barely holding on to her candle. Hot wax dripped onto her skin, making her draw in her breath with a sharp hiss. Another bang followed. Pistol shots?

How stupid she was to come here unaccompanied! What if the smugglers found her? She could disappear forever, her dead body ditched into the loch, with nobody the wiser. Had she really thought the cave was deserted, for her to snoop around at her pleasure? Clearly, it was not.

Oh, my God! What if a smuggler shot Rory and was on his way to the house to collect his dues? Or what if Rory killed another man? Fear gripped her throat like a man's hands.

Clasping the candle stump, she turned and picked her way back through gravel and rocks. Catriona cursed her insatiable curiosity. This time it took her too far.

Another sound made her look over her shoulder. The light at the end of the tunnel was growing brighter. A torch. It was moving toward her, still hidden from full sight by the turns of the path. Panic rose in her chest. Was the man coming after her going to kill her? And what if that man were Rory? After all, she'd discovered his secret.

She held her candle low to hide its flame, lifted her skirt and ran as fast as she dared on the uneven surface. Once she was safely around the sharp corner of the tunnel leading toward the house, she dared breathe a little. With all the twists and turns, she remained out of sight. Still, she best hurry.

Her feet were sore with stinging blisters, having bumped her toes into so many rocky outcrops she'd long lost count. Her head spun from running while concentrating on not banging into any overhanging ledges. The torchlight behind her loomed brighter. *Closer.* Another bend and she saw the opening to the fireplace. As the light from the library grew, she blew out her candle, biting her lip as hot wax dripped onto her fingers.

She dashed through the opening and for a moment contemplated pushing the lever to close the stone door. But the noise was bound to alert whoever followed her. Best to leave it as is. Ducking underneath the lintel, she raced for the door, but just as she tried to turn the stubborn key in the old lock, steps echoed on the stone floor of the fireplace. It was too late. In terror, she turned.

***

Rory stared at the sight that met him when he ducked out of the fireplace. He was right. Someone *had* followed him. A scent of lavender hung in the tunnel, betraying its owner. Not that lavender was the only proof of her presence. Looking Catriona up and down, he chuckled. Cobwebs stuck to her hair, soot smeared her cheeks, and dust covered the folds of her gown. She looked like she just squeezed through the chimney.

"My, look who we have here." He grinned. Then he pulled young Jamie out of the opening and bent back underneath the lintel to push the lever into place. The stone door slid back with a scrunching sound. It made her jump, and the smile on his lips died. This was serious.

"Jamie, sit." The lad did as he was bid, brushing off his clothes before carefully lowering himself on the edge of a leather armchair.

Catriona crossed her arms underneath her breasts, lifting them to reveal the creamy contours. Clearly, she was unaware of the effect. Rory swallowed hard. This was no time to consider the lady's ample accoutrements. She'd discovered his secret. He'd been so sure she'd never spot the lever, never dare dive underneath the lintel or into the suffocating, dusty darkness of the tunnel, that he'd not even considered the danger—both to herself and to him. He swore at his stupidity. She shrank back, bracing herself against the door, eyes wide.

Then his memory returned to the trouble in the cave, just before they'd made their way back. Had she heard the shots? Did she suspect him of shooting someone? Rory shook his head and gestured to another chair.

"Take a seat, Catriona," he ordered. When she stood rooted in place he strode over, took her arm, and led her to an armchair. She let him handle her without the least resistance. This was unlike her. Perhaps the enormity of her experience finally sank in.

Grudgingly, he found himself admiring her courage. Not many ladies of note ventured into dank, pitch-black tunnels. And with all that went on in there, 'twas no surprise she now felt the effects. He sighed, his tone softening. "My apologies, Catriona. But we need to talk."

"Y-y-yes," she stuttered, her voice barely above a whisper. *Damn!* He went over to the small side table and poured three glasses of brandy. They all needed it. He handed one to her and another to Jamie who sat in silence, watching his every move. Rory took a draught from his glass. What was he to do with her?

He leaned against the desk and stretched his legs out in front of him. Locking her eyes with his, he asked, "How did you find the tunnel?"

Her gaze darted to the fireplace, and then met his again, growing wide. "What tunnel?"

"Don't play daft with me, lass. I know where you've been." He pointedly looked her up and down, taking in the soot on her gown, her tresses falling wildly down her shoulders, then he reached out with his free hand to remove a cobweb from her hair. She flinched at his light touch.

How terrified she was! What exactly *had* she seen? He held out the cobweb. "You've been wandering around places you have no business knowing about. Why could you not keep your pretty nose out of it?" He wiped the cobweb on his trews and took another sip.

"I—" She swallowed.

"Drink!" He pushed the glass to her mouth. She coughed when the strong liquid hit her throat. Rory nodded. "Now tell me what you've been up to. Every little detail." Her gaze darted back to him, her face wary and guarded.

"Who's that?" She glanced at Jamie.

"This is Jamie, but you needn't concern yourself with him." From the corner of his eye he noticed Jamie was as flexed as a bow, ready to jump. A chivalrous youth out to defend the damsel in distress. Rory's patience was wearing thin. He emptied his glass and slammed it onto the desk.

"Catriona!"

She jumped and the words flew from her mouth. "I came in here for something to read and by chance found—"

"Stop lying to me, wench." Rory took a step toward her, towering over her as she shrank back into her chair. Leaning forward, his hands gripped the arms of the chair on either side of her. He hemmed her in, wanting to intimidate her. No, he must intimidate her. He cursed himself for having to do it, having to scare her, but if he didn't, she might put herself in danger.

"I was up late last night," she blurted out, "talking with Auntie Meg. About Edinburgh." She blushed and quickly took another sip.

He nodded. "And?"

"And after I took her to her room, I came back to extinguish the candles in the dining room, and secure the brazier. When I left the room, I heard a commotion. Well, at first I thought it was an intruder, then a ghost, coming out of the fireplace. But in the corridor, I recognized you."

"So you were hiding. Behind the oak cupboard?"

"Yes." She lowered her gaze and stared into the brown liquid in her glass. Her hands clung to it like to a lifeline, knuckles white with tension. "I'm sorry. I didn't mean to pry. 'Twas only because I was so scared."

He lifted her chin so their eyes met. Hers shone dark in the faint light of the room, a deep golden hue. For a moment, he forgot everything around him—time, place—all became non-existent, as he stared into the depths. The thoughts crossing his mind had nothing to do with intimidation. On the contrary, he wanted to haul her up and pull her into a tight embrace, reassure her, make her safe. With a sudden movement he stepped back from her chair. The golden pools widened. He saw fear. Fear of him?

"So you thought you'd spy on me?"

"No." Color rose in her cheeks. "I never meant to do that."

"Yes, you did." He strode to the window, his mind racing. He needed distance. The fog was even thicker than before, barely letting any light through. Gazing out, he said, "So you decided in your infinite boredom to discover whatever lay hidden. Tell me...are you that forthright in Edinburgh society?"

"How dare you!" He turned to find her standing, legs apart, hands balled into small, soot-blackened fists. Tears brimmed in her eyes as she glared at him. Oh, she understood his insinuation. Just as he'd intended. So why did it make him feel so wretched?

He watched her swallow hard, and lift her chin. "I'm sorry I followed my curiosity and searched for the door. I'm sorry I scrambled along a dank, filthy tunnel in near darkness. I'm sorry I've inconvenienced you and your...friend." She pointed at Jamie who sat staring at his feet. "I'm sorry I heard the shots..." Her eyes widened, too late realizing what she'd said. She shook her head. "But you have no right—"

"What shots?" he asked, his ragged emotions hidden. She must have been close enough to hear. But had she also been close enough to see? He'd spotted a faint light ahead of him in the tunnel after he left the cave but he was not absolutely certain it was her, until he found the stone door open, and her standing at the library door, looking like a treasure hunter, disheveled and grimy. And undeniably tempting.

"Nothing." Catriona looked at her hands fidgeting with the folds of her skirt. "No shots. Just a sound in the tunnel. Probably rats." Tears rolled down her cheek. She was lying again. She still suspected him. Looking at her shaking and scared, he wondered. No, she'd not seen the shooting.

Exasperated and angry with himself, he let out a long, slow breath. There had to be a way to ensure the girl did not interfere with his business again? If she'd made it to the cave and met one of his associates instead of him, she'd be fish fodder by now. Trussed up like Jamie, and thrown into the loch. The Jacobite cause was too fragile to risk on the whim of a nosy woman. He must find a way to keep her quiet—and away from his dealings, scared enough to never venture through the tunnel again. He looked at her tear-smudged face. Yes, this might work. He went to her, smiled, and took her hands between his.

***

Maybe she should run away.

Catriona didn't trust Rory. Not now, after what happened in the cave. His sudden quiet, friendly manner scared her more than the anger he controlled but moments earlier. She was certain he'd fired the shots. Looking down, she saw his hands bore faint traces of gunpowder. Yet here he was, soothing her with whispered words, stroking her grimy hands. He pulled another cobweb from her hair and shook it off.

"Catriona." He paused, softly wiping her tears away with his thumb. "Why don't you go upstairs and clean yourself up? When you've rested, this all will seem like a dream. I'm not angry with you. So don't worry." The smile never left his face, yet it reminded her of a cat, patiently waiting to pounce on an unsuspecting mouse. It did not reach his eyes. Her body continued to shake, and his thumb still caressed her cheek, trailing along her chin, tracing an imaginary line down her neck.

Catriona hardly dared breathe, the hairs at the back of her neck rose with every inch he covered. His gaze rested on her mouth. Nervously, she wet her lips with the tip of her tongue. Her mouth went dry under his scrutiny. The corners of his lips twitched, and for an instant she thought he was going to kiss her. Then he took a step back and released her.

"Until dinner, *mo chridhe*." He bowed and pointed at the library door. She was free to go. Still trembling, she fumbled with the key in the lock. Darned thing! She cursed herself for locking the door. Before she knew it he was behind her, his arms circling her waist, warm fingers strong on hers as they turned the key together. His breath hot on her neck, her heart skipped a beat.

Catriona jerked away from his hands and glared at him over her shoulder. As she opened the door, he stepped back, holding his hands up, the smile of a fox still on his face.

"Until later," he repeated.

Now she knew how a rabbit caught in a trap felt.

Without uttering a word, she ran upstairs, locked herself into her room, and collapsed against the door. What had she done? Surely now he'd have to silence her. This was supposed to be her sanctuary, her safe haven away from Angus and his machinations. Now she was in even graver danger—in danger for her life.

Her gaze fell on her travel dress hanging on the clothes peg, cleaned from the mud of her journey. A plan formed in her mind. She must not lose any time.

Chapter Eight

Auntie Meg entered the dining parlor, leaning heavily on her stick. Guilt rushed through Rory. With all of his thoughts on how to rid himself of Catriona he'd forgotten his aunt. He must make up for it.

He sauntered to the table and helped Auntie Meg settle in her chair. As he poured her a glass of wine, its heady scent filled the room. For one evening, he'd set aside his plans for Catriona's removal and focus on his home. Auntie Meg was going to enjoy tonight. His mind made up, he raised his glass.

"To family." He drank and the strong fumes relaxed him. This was potent stuff. His gaze met Auntie Meg's.

"To family, Rory." A smile played around her lips which she quickly hid as she sipped at her wine.

"What are you planning now?" He saw it in her eyes—the twinkle that heralded an idea. He hoped it didn't include Catriona. Thinking of the lass reminded him of the time. *Where was she?*

"Have you spoken to Catriona tonight?" He put his glass down.

Auntie Meg shook her head. "I haven't seen her since this morning. Why?"

"She's late."

"Oh." Auntie Meg glanced at the table clock on the sideboard. Dinner was due. "She may have fallen asleep."

At this moment, Mairi entered with a tray laden with steaming bowls of roast rabbit and root vegetables. She placed them on the table near Auntie Meg and looked around the room. Her quizzical gaze fell on Rory.

"Hasn't Catriona come down yet?"

"Clearly not." He was a little put out. Mairi's eyes held a

glint of accusation. "Can you fetch her?" Aware his voice sounded abrupt, he added, "Please."

Mairi nodded, then lay a hand on Auntie Meg's arm. "Please start, Lady Meg. Else it gets cold." Then she rushed from the room.

"Shall we?"

When Auntie Meg nodded, Rory took a serving spoon and filled her plate with meaty stew. He'd barely helped himself when Mairi burst into the room.

"She's gone!"

Rory jumped up, the back of his chair crashing against the sideboard. "What do you mean, gone?" He stared at her, an icy grip closing over his heart.

"I can't find her. She's not in her bedroom, nor in the kitchen, nor the library. She's disappeared."

"Nonsense! She can't just disappear. It's turning dark outside. Cat wouldn't be foolish enough to venture out at dusk. She has to be somewhere in the house." He righted his chair.

When Auntie Meg began to rise, he put his hand on her shoulder. "Don't fret, please. I'll search for her." The look of distress on her face tore at his heart. "I'll find her." He kissed her cold forehead and, ordering Mairi to stay with her, marched from the room.

The library was empty. No recent sign of anyone inside. He went over to the fireplace and pulled the lever. The stone door creaked open and darkness loomed ahead. No flickering candle in the distance.

"Catriona!" he barked, his voice echoing along the deserted tunnel. Only silence reached him when the sound subsided. She was not here.

Panic rose in his throat as he secured the door and stepped out of the fireplace. He shook off the dust and stalked toward the stairs. Taking two steps at a time, he ran to her bedroom and threw open the door.

Empty. Cold.

Guilt mingled with worry as he searched her room for clues. Her dresses hung on the clothes peg, and the bedcovers were neatly folded. As if she'd left. His blood froze. He found no trace of her cloak, or the riding boots she wore on her arrival. Surely the lass was not daft enough to head outside, with a chilly night closing in? He stared out of the window.

***

Catriona shivered in the evening breeze and pulled her cloak closer around her. Tears stung in her eyes as she kept her head high. She'd soon reach Baile a Chaolais and prayed a kind soul let her stay the night in their cottage. First thing in the morning, she'd take the ferry across and find a guide to take her...where? Where indeed? A sob racked her as loneliness pierced her heart. No-one wanted her.

Her toe hit a rock and she went flying, catching herself on knees and elbows. Pain seared through her limbs as the new scrapes on her shins and arms burned. Her fists hit the gravel as she cried out. Even the elements were against her.

She sat back, taking deep breaths. Once her breathing steadied, she stood. With trembling hands, she brushed the dust from her riding skirt and cloak. She must look presentable when she knocked on the crofters' doors.

Dusk settled over the loch as she marched on, away from *Taigh na Rhon*. Away from Rory. Night fell. It turned dark quicker than she expected. She glanced at the hilltops and frowned at the thick clouds gathering at the peaks. *Please don't let it rain.* She must hurry. Increasing her steps she ploughed along the path, careful not to trip again. The sharp edges of the stones stabbed at her feet. Not even the leather soles of her riding boots helped. Her feet ached, and she gritted her teeth against the pain. The village must be close by. She'd walked for miles. Or so it seemed.

A sudden gust of wind tore at her cloak and blew the hood from her head. Irritated, Catriona glared at the sky where the clouds had drifted deeper into the valley, hanging over the loch like a blanket. The breeze chilled her bones. She pulled the hood up again and tied her woollen scarf tighter around her neck. Rubbing her hands, she increased her steps, nearly running when the first drop of rain hit her heated cheeks. *Damn!*

She stopped and glanced around, looking for shelter. The birches and oaks provided scant cover. Cold drizzle drummed on her face when she spotted an abandoned hut further up the hill, with remnants of a thatched roof still in place. Making up her mind, she gathered her skirts and scrambled up the slope, her boots sliding on the damp grass. Her hands sought the trunks of the trees as leverage as she pushed her way uphill.

The heavens opened the moment she reached the croft. Gasping for air, she leaned against the solid stone wall before she snuck through the gaping hole that used to be the door. The roof was intact on the far side and she rushed toward its cover. She breathed a sigh of relief. Grateful for the shelter from the elements, she dropped down on the moss and heather covered floor. Exhaustion overcame her in waves, making her limbs heavy. She winced at the stinging pain in her feet as she stretched her legs. Her breathing slowed as she leaned back against the wall. When she pulled off her torn mittens and saw scratches covering her hands, tears streamed down her face, and loneliness washed through her. No-one wanted her. She was all alone.

What on earth was she going to do?

***

Rory swore. He stood outside *Taigh na Rhon* and scanned the landscape, the wind whipping his hair.

No sign of Catriona.

Mairi stopped next to him. "I don't understand, Rory. Where did she go?"

"I don't know." Fury raged inside him. At Catriona for running away, causing Auntie Meg to worry. At himself for making her. He'd scared her and now she'd fled. He turned to Mairi, pushing his guilt to the back of his mind.

Focus.

"Did she say anything to you?" he asked.

"No, but my bet is she's on her way home. Even though they don't want her."

He sighed. "That seems to be the problem. She's terrified of what might happen to her."

"Aye," Mairi said. "But why would she leave this time of day?"

He met her gaze, ignoring the suspicion in her eyes. With a final glance at the loch, he made up his mind. "I'll go after her. Have my horse saddled!" Hurrying, he grabbed his plaid from his clothes chest, his flintlock musket, stacked behind the door, and his gunpowder pouch. His gaze fell on the window. Seeing the clouds sink lower into the valley, he swiftly loaded his musket and, leaving it half-cocked, slung the metal strap over his shoulder, and wrapped himself into the plaid. He prayed he did not need to use the weapon.

"Best be prepared," he muttered as he shut the door behind him. Outside, a lad waited, holding the reins of Rory's favourite mare, Ish.

"Godspeed, Rory. Bring her home safe." The message in Mairi's eyes was unmistakable. She blamed him.

No wonder. He blamed himself.

"Wish me luck." He heaved himself into the saddle and spurred the mount along the path to the shore. Without a backward glance, he urged Ish on the lane to Baile a Chaolais. A fine drizzle settled on his skin as his gaze explored the hillsides. Not a soul in sight. Surely she'd have stayed on the path and not ventured from it uphill? The forests were teeming with wild animals. Worry and fear gnawed at his gut, leaving a bitter aftertaste in his throat. If anything happened to her...

He shook off his gloomy thoughts and focused on the path ahead. Only a couple of miles to go. Rain drenched him by the time he reached the settlement. No-one was out. He squinted his eyes and reined Ish in outside the first hut. He jumped from the saddle and banged his fist on the door.

"Open!" he bellowed against the howling wind.

The door creaked open a couple of inches and a pinched

face, lined and drawn, glared at him. Then the man relaxed and opened the door further. "Ruairidh? What brings ye out so late? Has aught happened to Lady Meg?"

"Sorry to disturb you, Stewart. Lady Meg's in good health but our visitor's missing. Have you seen a young lass today? Quite tall, dark hair?"

Stewart's eyes widened. "The lass from the ferry the other day?"

Rory nodded. "Aye, the same. She seems to have...gone walking." Heat shot into his cheeks. Hopefully the dim light hid it from the crofter.

"Nay, haven't seen her. Why d'ye think she's here?"

"She might want to go home to Edinburgh." Rory shuffled his feet. "You sure she hasn't been in the village?"

"Aye. We've all been oot today but seen no-one. Sorry, Ruairidh. Guess the lass might've taken cover?" Stewart glanced past him and Rory turned, the stiff breeze ruffling his hair. To his relief the rain stopped.

"You may be right. I'd best head back."

He turned and mounted, Ish's rump wet under his trews. He raised a hand and nodded. "Thank you, Stewart."

As the crofter closed the door, Rory urged Ish back onto the path. His breathing ragged, worry for Catriona's safety pushing him onwards. Steady! No need to rush.

He slowed Ish to a trot. The lass must be somewhere near. But the trees on the slope provided little shelter. He rode on, cursing his own stubbornness again. If he had not pushed the lass, she'd be safe at home.

His hopes plummeted as he rode on, his gaze drifting back and forth over the hillside, but he kept it away from the water. Cat was too clever to fall in. With a damp hand he shoved his hair from his face. His insides turned raw with fear.

A shadow loomed halfway up the hill, partly hidden by trees. He caught his breath as his heartbeat quickened. Of course, the abandoned croft! Rory let out a sigh of relief. That must be her hiding place. He jumped from the saddle and tied Ish's reins to a branch of a spruce.

Careful not to slip on the wet rocks, he climbed the slope until he came to a halt outside the gaping hole in the wall. What if she was not here? He swallowed hard.

Please.

For an instant he closed his eyes, then took a step over the threshold, ducking to avoid the low frame.

Adjusting to the dimness, he scanned the croft. "Catriona?" It came out as a whisper. He cleared his throat. "Catriona?"

"Rory?" A whimper came from a corner hidden under the roof in complete darkness.

He rushed over, nearly toppling over her outstretched legs. Relief flooded through him. He crouched next to her and gingerly wrapped her in his arms. "Catriona, are you all right?"

She nodded against his shoulder. "Y-y-yes." She sniffled, and let out a deep breath. Her hands clung to his arms and her body shook.

"Damn it," he swore and unpinned the brooch holding his plaid in place. He wrapped the thick blanket around her and pulled her to his chest. "You're safe now, mo chridhe." He closed his eyes and breathed in her scent of lavender and sea air. Her shivers slowed, and her body relaxed in his embrace. A sense of belonging invaded his mind, replacing the guilt. He touched his lips to her damp forehead.

"You're safe."

***

Rory paced the length of the drawing room. Hands fidgeting behind his back, he stopped and scowled at his faint reflection in the windowpane. His conscience never pricked him but it did now. Strange, as he most certainly did not care for her.

He refused to care for her.

Vigorously, he shook his head to rid himself of the conflicting thoughts. Seducing the lass only to make her leave was inexcusable. That was the reason she ran.

Was he such a fiend? It seemed so. She was a danger to the cause, a danger to him, her curiosity nearly killing her. But to flee into the approaching night, in utter disregard of her safety?

He scowled at his reflection. Shame washed through him, and he pulled the curtains to cover his image.

A sigh reminded him he was not alone. His gaze fell on Auntie Meg, reclining on the sofa with her eyes closed, her feet close to the brazier. The flames warmed the room yet still his body shivered. He'd nearly caused the lass to die.

Crossing to Auntie Meg, he adjusted the blanket over her thin body. She opened her eyes, and he read the accusation in them. "Don't fret, Auntie Meg. Catriona will be fine in the morning."

"It's a blessing you found her, Rory. We must discover what made her run and ensure it doesn't happen again." Her gaze bored through him, an eyebrow raised. "You wouldn't know a reason why Catriona wished to leave *Taigh na Rhon*?" When he shook his head, she closed her eyes. "'Twould pain me to see the two people dearest to my heart quarrel."

He winced, and went to sit in the armchair, resting his head against the cushioned back.

The minutes ticked by, the sound of the clock reverberating in his head as his mind whirled. He must find a way to keep Catriona safe and away from his business at the same time. Her returning to Edinburgh seemed like the only solution. Yet why did it feel like a loss?

When Mairi entered, he looked up. "How is she?"

"Warm and cozy, no thanks to you."

Irritated, he stood. "So you think *I'm* the reason she ran?"

Mairi huffed in frustration. "She wouldn't tell me. But neither Lady Meg nor I made her leave."

"I'm relieved to hear she's recovering," he growled as he brushed past her.

***

After a day's rest under Mairi's care, Catriona arrived early for dinner, only to find Rory and Auntie Meg already gathered. Their conversation stopped the moment she entered, and an uncomfortable silence fell. Had they been discussing her? She looked at her godmother—the heightened color in her face proof of some form of disagreement.

Heat rose in her cheeks as her gaze met Rory's. The memory of when he found her—how he held her close, whispering words of reassurance—came flooding back. He had saved her, brought her home.

Did he care for her?

Embarrassed, she rushed past him and took her godmother's hand. "Good evening, Auntie Meg. How are you feeling? Would you like me to pour you some wine?" She led the frail lady to her chair and helped her settle in.

"No, thank you, dear. I think I'll leave that to Rory." Her gaze was still on her nephew, a hint of question shining in her eyes.

"Of course, Auntie Meg." Rory strode over to the sideboard, poured the dark red liquid into a crystal glass, and handed it to Auntie Meg with a mock bow. "Happy to oblige." He filled Catriona's, an intense look in his eyes, sending delicious shivers down her spine. Then he strolled over to his chair and flopped onto it, stretching his long legs.

Catriona sighed inwardly. The sight of him wearing tight trews only led to thoughts of a scandalous kind. What if he'd worn a kilt? *Oh, dear Lord.* The memory of his legs, the soft light hairs sprinkled over sun-darkened skin holding those muscles into place came unbidden to her mind. She blinked and forced her attention to her godmother.

"You will enjoy dinner tonight, Auntie Meg. Cook has agreed to prepare a game pie, Mairi tells me. And did you notice the smell of fresh bread? She's been so busy, just to spoil us a little." She settled in her own chair, painfully aware of her incessant chattering, and prayed the old lady didn't notice her trembling hands. She kept her gaze strictly on her godmother, a wide smile on her face. A smile intended to hide her frayed nerves.

Rory sensed it, no doubt. She didn't dare glance at him. She must banish the memory, the light brush of his lips on her forehead, the tender care he took when he lifted her onto the back of his horse.

Now she knew why girls in their first season became infatuated with rakes. Of course, men had kissed her before, a few vain attempts by keen suitors, and her bastard of a former betrothed. But no-one came close to causing such sensations in her body. When Rory was with her, her insides whirled like wild waters. One look, one touch, and all propriety went out the window. He pulled her into depths she'd never experienced before. And perhaps even more dangerous, after last night, he made her feel safe.

How ironic, after she'd thought he meant her harm! Instead, he came to her rescue, proving her foolish thoughts wrong.

He glanced at her, their gaze meeting. For a long moment he held it. Too long. Catriona averted her eyes and interlaced her fingers in her lap.

When dinner was served, Catriona made up her mind to ignore Rory, and focus on her food instead. She involved Auntie Meg in a conversation about the old lady's health. A safe topic. Just as long as she did not risk a glance toward Rory who remained silent.

Her skin tingled as she felt his gaze on her throughout the meal, and she caught her godmother watching him. The tension in the air was palpable.

The dishes removed, silence fell once more as they sipped their port.

"I'm tired," Auntie Meg announced after finishing her drink. "But before bed I'd like a minute alone with Catriona."

Catriona held her breath, hoping Rory would find an excuse to stay.

But he dashed her hopes.

"Of course. I have papers that require my attention." Rory stood in the door, his eyes resting on his aunt. "I wish you a good night." Then the door closed behind him.

"Now, dearie," Her godmother turned to her. "I wish to know what sent you out into the night yesterday. I was so concerned about you. We all were."

Catriona focused on her hands clenched in her lap. What could she say? She had been scared of Rory? She expected him to harm her? No, she must find a quick excuse although the suggestion of lying to Auntie Meg hurt her.

"I was…erm…confused."

"Confused?" Auntie Meg's eyes blazed. "What does that mean, child?"

Catriona's mind whirled. "'Tis nothing to worry about. I just wasn't sure I was still wanted here."

"Catriona MacKenzie!" Auntie Meg's voice held a stern note. "This is ridiculous. Of course you're wanted here. Now tell me what happened to give you such foolish thoughts."

Catriona looked down at her hands in her lap. Finally, she met her aunt's gaze once again. "I'm sorry to have caused you such worry, Auntie Meg."

"Did Rory have anything to do with it?" The question came like a shot.

"Rory? Certainly not." She prayed her godmother did not notice the tremble in her voice. "Why do you think so?"

"Just a feeling I have. You see, I've been watching you two, pacing like a pair of lions around each other. Something must have occurred." Her face softened yet the determination was still clear in her eyes.

"With everything that happened back home, and coming here, I've just been a bit confused. It was silly of me to run away." *And that was all she would say.*

"I wouldn't calling risking my life silly but so be it." Auntie Meg sighed. "I shall have to make up my own mind."

Catriona jumped up as her godmother stood. She handed her the walking stick and turned away from the table, to help her to her room. "No thank you, Catriona. I'll manage just fine on my own. Mairi will be at hand to assist. I wish you sweet dreams."

With a final glance at her, Auntie Meg shuffled into the corridor. Mairi's voice reached her, assuring her she'd take care of the old lady.

Catriona's cheeks burned, and she was suffused with shame. She sat and rested her hot face in her hands. How could she lie to her godmother? Yet, Auntie Meg would never accept the truth.

Much to her embarrassment, Rory appeared, closed the door, and turned. Leaning back, one booted foot against the wood, he crossed his arms.

"Finally we're alone," he said, his eyes unreadable. "I've been watching you, Cat. You're still not yourself. Are you not fully recovered yet?" He strolled back toward the table, rounded it, and came to a halt in front of her. Her mouth went dry.

Resting his hip against the back of a chair next to hers, his gaze roamed her body. Heat of a different kind flooded back into her cheeks as, at leisure, his gaze rested at her exposed neck, her breasts, rising and falling too fast for her liking, and her hips. She tried to slow her breathing. The intensity in his eyes made her feel exposed. Naked.

She swallowed, her feet frozen to the spot, her mind blank. *Do something*! Because she did not want to brush against him —which she'd have to if she passed him—she sat back down. Immediately, she realized her mistake. For now her eyes were level with his flat stomach and narrow hips, the tight trews pronouncing his masculinity. *Dear Lord!*

The heat in her cheeks grew deeper, and she lowered her gaze. Her fingers linked tightly, she felt like a naughty child. No, not a child. The sensations coursing through her body were most definitely not childlike. Rather like Eve tempted by the apple, with Rory as Adam.

Rory lifted her chin with his hand, his forefinger resting underneath while his thumb stroked her lips. "Are you still afraid, *mo chridhe*?" The soft Gaelic lilt sent a delicious shiver down her spine. "Because if you are, there's no need."

He took her hands and pulled her up against him.

"As I said last night, you're safe."

Any wriggle to free herself from his grasp only brought her closer. Her legs parted to the pressure of his thigh, her hands found themselves nestled against his chest.

A warm sense of belonging spread through her. Once again, she was safe.

Underneath his linen shirt, his heartbeat increased against her palm, flexed muscles tempting her fingers to explore. Nudged by him, she gave in, her arms making their own way around his neck. Resistance was pointless. A sigh escaped her as his hands slid down her back, pulling her even tighter against him. Her breasts, confined under the rigid surface of her stays, pushed against his chest. The rush of excitement, so new and forbidding, made her head spin.

He brushed her mouth with his before his lips moved across to the sensitive spot under her earlobe, further down her neck, leaving a trail of soft, hot kisses in their wake. He nudged the border of her gown off her shoulders with his teeth and nibbled at the exposed flesh. Another sigh escaped her, lost in the rush of blood in her ears.

"Catriona."

Rory's hand moved over her hips, inch by inch upwards to her breasts. A sweet dizziness came over her as his fingers slid into her stays and caressed the sensitive skin. When his thumb brushed over her hardening nipple, she whimpered.

Her gasp was instantly crushed by a kiss very different from any that came before. Rory's mouth was hard on hers, his tongue demanding entry into unexplored territory. She opened her lips to allow him in and he took full control, reaching deep inside to nudge her tongue to respond. The thrill was tearing her apart, her skin tingling, her brain numb. Following an unknown instinct, she pulled his head even closer as her heart pounded to bursting point.

Catriona shuddered with the unexpected pleasure of it, her breathing ragged. His hardened shaft pushed against her and she shifted her legs as if by silent demand. He moved between her thighs, one hand on her bottom to pull her tighter. The pressure melted her lower regions into sweet dampness, making her body writhe as he rubbed against her. With the last of her reserve gone, she explored his mouth with a hunger matching his, their kiss an endless game of tempting and responding. Unable to resist, she clung to him as his hands roamed over her exposed skin, her body softening against his.

Then Rory broke the kiss.

"Rory," she whispered. When he didn't reply, she opened her eyes and found him staring. Startled at the intensity in the dark green, unreadable pools, she tried to make sense of his abrupt withdrawal.

He took a step back, and ran his hands through his ruffled hair. "I'm sorry, Catriona."

Her body shivered but not with excitement. Bereft of something she could not name, a chill settled on her still hot skin. She rushed past him to the window, trying to control her breathing, her whirling emotions. She grabbed the windowsill for support and leaned her forehead against the glass, cooling her burning skin. Tears stung behind closed eyelids. What had she done?

"This has gone too far. I can explain—"

She forced out the words, "I don't want to hear it."

His steps on the wooden floor came closer until she felt the heat from his body behind her. His hands hovered over her arms but he withdrew without touching her.

"This is hard for me. It's not you."

"I know it's not me. It never is." Her voice wobbled. She was right back in the rain-swept cottage. All alone.

"I...I have to focus on the cause. We, the Jacobites, are about to organize another rising, and anyone associated with me—" He stopped, looked away as if choosing his words carefully. "You're in danger if we go on like this. I can't risk it." His voice broke, his warm breath brushing her neck. "I'm sorry."

Tears pricked her eyes but she didn't turn around. "So am I."

"'Tis for the best. But I'd still like to show you the manor. Auntie Meg would wonder if I didn't."

She nodded, her mind hollow. "Yes, we should go on as if nothing happened." Unable to hide the bitterness in her voice, she added, "After all, nothing *has* happened."

He stepped back. Cold air engulfed her. "Be ready tomorrow after breaking your fast. We're going to take a boat out on the loch." His voice held a ragged note.

She heard him pour some wine and put the decanter back on the sideboard. "I wish you sweet dreams." His footsteps stopped at the door, and he opened it. "Oh, and please stay away from the library at night. I don't want you to meet any danger." As silence descended—only interrupted by the ticking of the clock—tears streamed down her face.

***

Catriona came to his bed unbidden. Her thick tresses tumbling over her shoulders, she wore nothing but a thin, silken nightdress. In the candlelight, he saw her taut nipples, dark behind the sheer fabric. The curly triangle between her thighs called out for his touch. Smiling, she leant over the edge of the bed, and he shifted to make way for her, his arms stretched out to pull her close.

She slid into his embrace, her hair brushing softly over his naked chest. Slender fingers caressed the outlines of his muscles, leaving a trail of tingling skin. Her full mouth lowered to follow where her fingers led. Rory leaned back, his hands catching the long, thick waves of her hair. Her fingers reached the throbbing heat of his erection and encircled him in a firm grip. His fingers lost hold of her hair as her head moved to follow her hands.

"Cat!" Rory gasped as he opened his eyes, his hands reaching into empty space.

Faint light filtered through the curtains. He was alone. Swearing, he kicked the bedcovers off to cool his burning body. His cock was throbbing for release. He turned to the side and pulled up his knees, cursing himself for allowing Catriona to take control. Despite the very real danger she'd be in if they grew too close, he found himself aching for her touch, wanting to take care of her.

He turned away from the window. She was probably still asleep now. Why had he agreed to take her out? He'd have to keep tight rein over himself. Giving in was too much of a risk. She already invaded his mind more often than he thought sensible.

He rose from the bed and stepped to the window. The early morning sun was already rising over the hills. The water of the loch lay in semi-darkness, as the sun's rays touched the peaks of the hills on the western shore. Like long, slim fingers, the rays traveled slowly down the slopes. He stood and watched, mesmerized by the awakening of nature. He loved spring in the Highlands.

When the light touched the water, sending shimmering ripples across the surface, he turned. He dipped his hands into the bowl on a side table, remembering the morning Catriona caught him washing himself in the kitchen. Since then, his instructions to Mairi were clear—a fresh bowl of water was to be left in his room every night.

The coolness invigorated his skin, still burning from the dream. Trews seemed more appropriate for a boat trip than a kilt. Should he fall into the water, the thick fabric of the kilt would pull him under.

Boots in hand, he tiptoed down the stairs to the kitchen. Surprised at sounds coming so early from the room—Cook hated early mornings—he pushed the door open an inch and peeked through. The view that met him made him grin.

The lad Jamie sat on a stool at the large table, a bowl of steaming porridge in front of him. Mairi stirred the thick liquid with a wooden spoon before handing it over to him. As their hands brushed, they giggled.

Rory coughed and pushed the door wide open. Jamie's sheepish expression and the maid's blushes made him laugh out loud. "You're up early, my lad." He walked over and ruffled the boy's hair, amused by the sudden red coloring of Jamie's cheeks. "Don't mind me. I'm just passing."

He grabbed an apple from a bowl on the table, and walked out the kitchen door into the yard. Once outside, he bit into the fruit, holding it with his teeth, and leaned against the wall to pull on and secure his boots. The sun had yet to cross the peaks, and the sky was a clear, light blue. There was nothing better than an early morning walk along the heather. Taking another bite, he munched as he walked behind the house to climb the hill. The full sunrise was best enjoyed from the top.

Chapter Nine

Several hours later, the sun high in the sky, Rory returned to collect Catriona for their scheduled boat trip. He'd meant to banish her from his mind, but instead found his thoughts wandering to the vision of her waking up in bed. Of course, his mind then veered off to her curves, most likely clad in nothing but the silky dream he'd seen her wearing that first morning. His body reacted to the picture with violent longing, which took him some time to suppress.

But he reaffirmed his intentions. Catriona must never be more to him than his aunt's goddaughter. Any closeness only led to danger. To her, and to him.

Now, having searched the drawing room, parlor and kitchen, he was about to give up when he heard a female voice humming the melody of a Gaelic lullaby. Following its origin, he pushed open the door to the library. She sat reclined in an armchair, legs tucked underneath her skirts, reading. At the sound of the door opening, she raised her head and smiled.

"Good morning, Rory. Lovely day, isn't it?"

"Good morning, Catriona. You're up early." His hand on the door, he watched as she put the book aside and rose, sliding her stocking-clad feet into her slippers. He found watching her unnerving, yet compulsive. This was dangerous ground. She'd been upset when he left her the night before, but now she seemed cheerful. The hairs on his neck stood on end, a tingling reached down his spine. What changed?

"I hope it's not too much trouble, taking me out on the loch." Her gaze sought his, her smile all temptation. Silently, he cursed himself for even agreeing to this endeavor.

"No trouble at all, as I said last night." He saw her flinch.

Ah, she was not as composed as she wanted him to believe. He gestured toward the corridor. "Shall we?"

A waft of lavender engulfed him as she strolled past and led the way out of the house. He followed with grim resolve. This was already proving trickier than he expected.

***

Leaning back, the breeze cool on her face, Catriona let her gaze drift across the rugged landscape. Wild flowers, just come into bloom, dotted the hillsides, their petals forming a colorful blanket on the steep slopes. What would it feel like to lie back on that blanket, inhaling the sweet scent of the flowers?

Rory interrupted her contemplation. He brought in the oars and pointed a finger to the far shore. "On that side lie Macdonald lands." He frowned and extended his hand in a wide gesture toward the shore they left earlier. "All this here is Cameron land. Our estate reaches well beyond the peak behind the manor, a few miles up the loch—far behind that corner there—and down to Baile a Chaolais."

He turned back to face her. As he dipped the oars into the water again and continued to row, the boat rocked a little. Soon, they lost sight of the house. Only the peak, rising high above the surrounding crests, reminded them of its location. The hill drifted farther and farther away as Rory pushed the boat northwards.

She took in the expanse of the estate, surprised at how much Auntie Meg owned, then watched Rory. His upper body moved with the flow of the boat, his biceps rippling to the rhythm of the oars.

Did he expect to inherit it all? If he did, surely he'd not be pleased about her growing closeness to Auntie Meg.

Perhaps there was some truth in her suspicion that Auntie Meg intended to marry them off to each other? The wily old lady certainly made much of them spending time together. After all, he was a fine example of a Highlander.

She let her gaze roam idly over the muscles, busy at work

under the tight linen shirt; the uncovered, tanned neck; the strong legs pushing against a plank for momentum. The memory of his kisses came unbidden. Her cheeks heated, and she averted her gaze toward *terra firma*, only to spot a strange rocky outcrop on the shore.

"What's that?" She pointed her finger, intrigued. Was this the entrance to his cave? A heightened sense of direction made her certain.

Rory grunted. "Just a lump of rock overhanging the water." He pulled the oars in, letting the boat bounce on the waves. Turning over, he pointed to a hut on the far shore. The roof was long gone, the shutters swayed in the wind.

"This is where the Redcoats caught a number of our men after the rebellion five years ago." He looked her in the eye. "They were taken outside and shot. No trial for common folk. No defense. No chance." He snorted. "The soldiers threw their bodies into the loch."

Catriona shivered as if a cold hand touched her. She stared into the dark depth, almost expecting to see a corpse appear from beneath the surface.

Rory laughed, a dry sound bereft of humor. "No worries, lass. Our clan pulled them all out after nightfall. The men received a proper burial, if naught else." His eyes, hard as flint, searched her face. What he was looking for, she did not know.

"I'm sorry," she said.

Any other words were pointless, fake. She wanted to reach out and take away the pain in his eyes, smooth the harsh lines that settled on his face the moment he told her of the fate of his clansmen.

She saw the raw anger and grief hidden inside him, suppressed for years, but never fully conquered. This was the first time he allowed her such a close glimpse at his feelings. She leaned forward, barely aware of the rocking boat, and took his hands between hers. His sudden, direct gaze scorched her.

"Are you?" His tone was cynical, his mouth twisted into a cruel smirk. "After all, Miss Catriona MacKenzie was safely tucked away in a big, luxurious house in the city. Far away from the troubles, from the poverty, from desperation." He jerked his hands from her grasp and knelt in front of her, pulling her toward him. He buried his fingers in her hair and brought her to her knees. "But I was there. I saw brave men killed and helpless women and children slaughtered. I fought. And I lost."

He swallowed. The boat rocked but she hardly noticed. His eyes held a gleam she found impossible to escape.

"How...how did you survive?" She caught her breath as his gaze darkened even further.

"Auntie Meg's connections and luck. They lacked proof of my involvement. As the heir to her estate, I was to be tried, and not just shot. After they arrested me in Inverness, I managed to escape en route to the Edinburgh goal and went into hiding. Two years later Auntie Meg sent me a message saying it was safe to come home. To this day, I don't know how she did it, how she got the Redcoats off my back. She never mentions that time. I'll be forever in her debt."

Their bodies but inches apart, her heart was pounding in her ears. With shaking hands, she touched his face.

"I can't help my upbringing, Rory, can't change my background. But I can empathize with—"

He glowered at her, their breath mingling. "Are you really saying you understand poverty? I bet you sat in your plush parlor, gloating with your friends about the misfortune of those stupid Catholics up north. Little Miss know-it-all!" He pushed away from her, bitterness apparent in every move.

"Yes, I *can* understand." She was close to losing her patience. Why did he not believe her? "I've seen misery. I've been to the poorhouses. And before you say it—no, not to boast about it to my friends, only to help. I was appalled by the injustice of it all." The skepticism in his gaze did not diminish. "Oh, believe what you like!"

But she could not take her gaze from his face, twisted with emotions he'd probably deny even feeling. His breathing was harsh with anger, and he watched her with an intensity she didn't understand.

As moments passed, the anger turned to hunger. Catriona remembered the pact they made the night before, to keep away from each other. But she could never deny him when he was hurting.

"Rory—" she began but then his mouth came down hard on hers, and Catriona parted her lips without thinking, abandoning herself to the emotions raging within him. He pushed her onto the hard boards, his tongue searching hers in a battle neither could win.

She flailed for a moment, sure the boat was going to capsize, but Rory managed to keep it from overturning, maintaining the balance with his knees as he moved on top of her. The hard planks hurt her back but she ignored the pain, allowing him to move a leg between hers.

When her skirts hampered him, he pulled them above her knees. Rough hands roamed her body, pulling at the stays covering her breasts. The cool breeze on her burning skin fanned her desire. He lowered his head to one and licked the sensitive skin around her nipple. It hardened even more when he pulled it between his teeth, his tongue flicking around it.

Catriona gasped, her body twisting beneath his. Any notion of resistance melted away. Her hands loosened his shirt and slid underneath, caressing hot skin. Her fingertips brushed the welts of scars across his back and her heart reached out even more. What had he endured during that failed uprising?

She rested her hands above his heart, taking in the strong, steady beat. A comforting beat. Sure and certain as the light of day.

Her breathing quickened as his hand moved to stroke her thigh, sending goosebumps over her skin. His thumb caressed the inside, kneading its way higher, until he pushed the hem of her sark over her hips. Her eyes flew open and she met his gaze, clouded with need.

Her hand clasped his and held it from moving any closer to her. He was going too far, too fast.

"Cat," he whispered, bringing his mouth close to her ear. His teeth nicked her lobe and she closed her eyes, delighting in the sensation.

No! She must stop him.

But when his fingers stretched from her grasp to touch the soft skin between her legs, she gasped. Her body betrayed her good sense, as shivers ran through it in waves. His thumb nudged closer until it found her most sensitive spot.

She moaned, shaking her head to match the rhythm of his thumb rubbing against her. He sent her body into spasms she'd never dared dream of. Unable to tear herself away from his touch, she gave in, allowing her body and mind to dissolve.

***

Catriona's kisses sent shivers down Rory's spine. The trace of her hands left a scorched trail of pins and needles all over his body. His mind told him to overpower her, to lose himself in her. She'd never understand his pain. Her body moved beneath his, legs wrapped around him, pulling him closer. Any self-control he possessed—no, he thought he possessed—was slipping away fast.

He let his tongue roam over the sensitive flesh of her neck, her breasts, sampling the sweet taste of a small, puckered nipple.

Not content with simply devouring her, he sent his finger into her soft core, rubbing and nudging the damp flesh, driving her to writhe in abandon. Aye, this was how he wanted her, completely depending on him, dependent on his touch. She raised her hips against his, tantalizing him, tempting him to take her. The need to remove his straining trews and push himself deep inside her, to take her with him on that final, ecstatic journey, was overpowering. Was she aware of what she was doing to him?

Was she aware of what she was doing?

He raised his head and looked at her. An innocent beauty lay beneath him, quivering from the exertion. Her long hair let loose, the tresses lay spread out across the planks. Her breasts, the rosy peaks so invitingly close to his mouth, tempted him to distraction.

Her face shone in pleasure.

Rory swallowed hard. What was he doing? Was he really seducing this girl on a boat, simply out of lust? Shame washed over him like an autumn flood. He meant only to show her the estate, not take out his needs on an innocent girl.

He kept watching her as he sat back and pulled his knees up. "We need to move on."

Her eyes fluttered open and she looked around, as if in a daze. They finally met his and he watched them change from delight to sadness. He reached out to help her steady herself but she flinched. Suddenly aware of her disheveled state, she scrambled to the far end of the boat, pulling her skirts tightly around her legs and covering her breasts.

"Why did you...?" Her cheeks turned crimson. Quickly, she lowered her gaze onto her folded arms and shut him out.

"I must apologise again, Catriona. 'Tis better this way. Safer. Trust me."

His heart mourned the loss, and his body ached with unfulfilled desire, but his mind was relieved. Perhaps she was one step closer to leaving. Then she'd be safe from the dangers lurking in the Highlands. And from him.

Rory swore as he grabbed the oars and shoved the ends into the water. Ignoring the splash, he turned the boat and aimed for the boathouse. Looking around, he searched the lands for signs of any spies. His mouth set, he kept his gaze away from her. How could he put himself—and her—at risk, straight into a potential firing line? He must be mad.

He was still tying the ropes of the boat when she slipped past him out of the boathouse without another word. After a final tug he rose, left the shed, securing the door behind him.

Ahead in the distance he saw her walking at a brisk pace. Her back straight, head thrown back with scant regard of her hair flowing wildly down her back. The breeze caught the burnished ends, tumbling them in her wake. He longed to catch them, to touch the softness, to let the tangled mass run through his fingers. It was pointless. He shoved his hands into his pockets and shook his head. Slowly, he began his walk back to the house. He needed to pack. And he needed to banish Catriona from his mind.

Once inside the house, he searched for Jamie. Not surprisingly, he found him in the kitchen. Rory chuckled. Something was going on with Mairi. The girl's cheeks were flushed as she busied herself washing cabbage.

"Sorry to interrupt this small gathering. Again." He became serious. "Jamie, we have to leave."

The boy jumped from his stool, his gaze darted from Rory to Mairi and back.

"What...now?"

Rory nodded. "Aye, now. We're due to meet an associate in two days' time and we've much to do beforehand. Can you gather your things and get the horses saddled? We'll leave as soon as we've packed." Turning to Mairi, he added, "Prepare some bread and cheese, if you will. Plenty of it. The journey may be long."

He left them to their preparations and headed upstairs to his bedroom. Stopping outside Catriona's closed door, he heard her swear. Something solid was thrown against the wall and he jumped. Another item followed at quick pace. My, the girl had a temper—and he'd unleashed it. He stared at the door. What would it be like to harness that temper into passion? He remembered her reaction to his kiss on the boat, her wild abandonment.

Stop! It must never happen again.

Determined to focus on the cause instead of the lass, he walked to his room and slammed the door behind him. Best nobody watched him pack his bags. Best nobody witnessed his fury.

***

Catriona threw herself onto the bed, her rage exhausted. She'd just thrown two precious books against the wall, and loose pages now scattered the floor. She'd done it again. Why was she so weak? She'd allowed Rory to entice her. And again, she'd reacted to his touch like a lost soul to light. He triggered feelings deep inside her she never knew existed. Was it like this between husband and wife?

Frowning, she imagined her parents, the stern father and withdrawn mother, in their bedroom. Surely, they'd never have done things like that? She sighed. No, Father was too formal to indulge in such passions. But perhaps Mother had dreamed of them before she wed.

She remembered her vivacious mother during her younger years, dancing and chatting gaily, excited with life. Such a contrast to the subdued and quiet lady her mother had become, all life drained from her. A wave of sympathy nearly choked her. How different Mother's life might have been if she'd caught a more sensitive husband.

Catriona let her hands rest on her chest. Her breathing quickened at the thought of Rory's touch, right where her hands lay now. What he'd done was unforgivable, yet how could she blame him? She'd been complicit in their deed, a willing partner to Rory's demands. The memory of his lips, the flicks of his tongue on her skin made her shiver.

Her fingertips brushed over her hardened nipples and she gasped. Was this wonderful feeling really such a bad thing? If so, why did she feel so free, so happy when he lay on top of her, his own excitement pressing against her, his mouth covering hers with such passion? So different than with John, who made her feel nothing but disgust with his sloppy kisses? With Rory, she'd felt like bursting with joy.

Placing her hands firmly on the sheets, Catriona sat up. What on earth was she thinking? Of course, it was bad. Even more so, it was most improper. She'd been compromised— *again*—but this time she'd been caught up in the passion.

Rory felt it, too, however much he denied it. She swallowed hard. Was she in love with Rory Cameron? And, more to the point, did he reciprocate her feelings?

She doubted that very much. Lust, perhaps, but never love. The man was a rogue, little better than a cattle thief or common smuggler.

If she was really in love, what hope did she have?

When his boots sounded on the floorboards outside her

door, Catriona stayed still. His steps headed for the stairs. Well, she'd just stay in her room. And tonight, she'd confront him. Tell him what went on inside her head. Then the next step would be up to him.

Her future was in his hands.

Chapter Ten

Catriona sat by the fire, browsing through a book about Greek mythology. It should have helped distract her from Rory but instead the tales of unrequited love, revenge, and death reminded her more than ever of what he'd endured. Despite the warmth of the fire, she shivered. Of course, she'd heard rumors about mass killings by soldiers, blithely ignored by the Edinburgh establishment.

Father, as an eminent member of society, attended executions of so-called traitors. He always made a point of voicing his opposition to the rebellion. Strangely, Mother remained silent on the issue, slowly withdrawing from her husband, and her children.

Catriona straightened, closing the book with a snap. Of course, that was it! The reason Mother retreated from the outside world. Clan Macdonald had been a major supporter in the rebellion, and her mother's loyalty to her Highland roots must run deep, even if she was not allowed to show it openly.

She should have talked to Mother, should have tried to understand her. Even more so as Father and Angus never cared to bother. Catriona leaned back and closed her eyes. As soon as she returned she'd speak to her.

When the door opened, she startled but did not turn. Fully expecting Rory to enter, she intended to give him the cold shoulder.

"Ah, there you are, dearie," Auntie Meg said as the end of her walking stick hit the floor. "You ready for supper?"

Catriona jumped up and helped her godmother into her chair. "Are you comfortable, Auntie Meg?"

"Aye, don't fret. Be seated yourself."

Catriona took her seat just as Cook entered with bowls of steaming rabbit stew and freshly baked bread.

Hesitating, she watched her godmother begin to break her bread. "Should we not wait for Rory?"

The old lady shook her head. "Nay, Catriona, eat away. Rory won't be joining us tonight. He had to go away." She dunked her bread into the thick stew, seemingly oblivious to Catriona's surprise.

Catriona stared at her. "What do you mean?"

"Just as I said. At times, Rory disappears. It's his own business he's looking after." She smirked as she looked quizzically at Catriona. "I never ask, and he never tells me. Better that way."

"Better?" Catriona was indignant. The coward! "You mean better for him? He wanders off, leaving you to pick up the work on the estate, and you say it's fine?" Her hands were shaking. Following her godmother's example she broke off a chunk of her bread. Yet she didn't taste a thing. Her mind was numb. Where was he? And why did he leave without telling her?

Auntie Meg laid a cold hand on hers and held fast. "Catriona, lass. You'll soon learn about the Highland ways. The longer you stay the better you'll understand. Rory has business of his own to attend to, and if we don't know what it is, then no government agent can force it from us."

Catriona blanched at the revelation. She remembered what Rory told her about the men who were shot. What if his activities brought him to the same end? The thought made her sick, and she took a deep breath to steady herself before she grabbed Auntie Meg's hand in return. "Why—?"

"Lassie, Rory Cameron's his own man. He makes his own decisions. I don't meddle, and neither will you. That way we're safe." The old lady squeezed her hand and continued eating as if they'd been chatting about the weather.

"What about him? Who's going to keep him safe?"

"My nephew can take care of himself."

Catriona's appetite vanished so she pushed her plate away. Ignoring Auntie Meg's raised eyebrow, she grabbed her glass of wine and took a deep draught of the ruby liquid. Its strength immediately went to her head. Her mind drifted back to the tunnel. She must go back into the tunnel—all the way to the cave this time, to see what he kept hidden there. Only then would she know the full extent of the danger he was in. After all, someone must keep Rory safe. Her mind made up, she smiled at Auntie Meg. "Apologies, Auntie, but I've no appetite."

"My, you've hardly eaten today. I knew it was too soon for you to take a trip on the loch. It seemed such a bonnie day but you can never be sure with those winds out on the water."

Her hand touched Catriona's forehead. "You've no fever. Maybe it's just the fresh sea air, though that usually has the opposite effect." She smiled.

"Thank you, Auntie Meg, but I've not caught the chills. I'm just not hungry." Auntie Meg's gaze searched her face. For what, she did not know.

"Oh, aye, dearie. Aye." Her godmother lifted her own glass, yet her gaze never left Catriona's face. "Did Rory behave himself today?"

Catriona's cheeks burned. Her gaze went toward the window. "I don't know what you mean. I've no complaints about him."

"You haven't, have ye? I've never seen him leave in such a haste. Strange, that." Her godmother's gaze bored into her.

Catriona shifted, embarrassed by the scrutiny. Had she guessed or seen something? Surely they'd been too far north on the loch. She looked up and met the appraising gaze. "I...I wish to retire now," she said, her voice hoarse. "With your permission, of course."

Auntie Meg leaned back and sighed. "So he did misbehave."

"I didn't say..." Catriona wanted to defend herself, but words failed her.

"You didn't have to, lassie. Your body replied on your behalf." She sat up. "Let me tell you one thing about Rory Cameron, Catriona. He never does anything without a reason. If he took advantage of you today, it's because he has feelings for you. Else he wouldn't have dreamed of touching you. You're not the type for a quick dalliance, he knows that. But what about you?"

Catriona covered her face with her hands and cried. "Oh God, I...Please excuse me, Auntie Meg."

Scrambling to her feet, she fled the room. She grabbed her skirts and raced up the stairs. Once inside her bedroom, she locked the door. She didn't want anybody to disturb her. Tears running down her face, Catriona threw herself onto her bed. What had she done? Now, Auntie Meg knew about her feelings. And she knew Rory seduced her, yet she'd not condemned either of them.

Oh, what a mess!

***

Rory pulled the collar of his greatcoat tighter around his neck. The winds were too strong here in the mountains. The relentless rain trickled underneath his collar, the rivulets running down his back. He looked across at Jamie. The lad was as soaked as he was and hunched into a similar position, crouched low on the back of his horse. Rory wiped the water from his eyes with the back of his hand and surveyed the area. In the distance, he saw a light flicker. Not far to go. Just as well. Night was closing in fast. He spurred his mount into a canter. Soon they'd be under a dry roof, well, partially dry. He heard Jamie spur his horse forward, and together they covered the couple of miles in little time.

They slowed when the crumbled walls of the abandoned hut loomed ahead. The thatch on most of the roof was gone, only a corner gave meager shelter. Still, any shelter was preferable to this constant drizzle. Rory dismounted and threw his reins to Jamie. "Tie the horses to that copse of trees over there."

He ducked underneath a low doorframe and entered what used to be the living space of a family of cattle drovers. In the dry corner covered by the roof, a small fire burned brightly, flames rising high when the odd gust of wind hit it.

The old man beside it looked up. "Ye took yer time, Ruairidh."

"I was held up." Rory dropped to the beaten ground as close to the fire as possible, crossing his legs in front of him. He rested a cool gaze on Auld Cameron. "Jamie MacKinnon's with me."

The other man looked up, a frown between his bushy brows. "Jamie? Why the hell—?"

"Because it's time, Cameron. That's why. He's keen to learn, and you nearly killed him when you trussed him up." Rory leaned forward and rubbed his hands close to the warming flames. He looked up as Jamie hovered in the door. "Come on over, lad, and warm yourself. Auld Cameron here doesn't bite. Well, not tonight."

"That's what you say, sir." Jamie mumbled but came over, huddling close to Rory, eyeing the other man suspiciously.

"Greetings, Jamie lad. Didna expect ye here."

"I didn't expect to be tied up either, Mr Cameron." The glint in the boy's eyes made Rory chuckle.

"Steady, lad! I'm sure Auld Cameron's sorry he trussed you up like he did." His gaze found the old man's and his smile vanished. "Aren't you, Cameron?"

The drover flinched. Rory's icy stare made him shuffle uncomfortably. "It was a jest, Ruairidh. How did I know he couldna free himself?"

"You might've checked on him. But instead..." Rory paused, his gaze not leaving the old man's face, "I find you gone without word. Why?"

"Well, ye ken what it's like, with all the Redcoats on the wa'er." The drover's hands fidgeted with a bunch of dead leaves scattered about. His gaze lowered, he refused to meet Rory's eyes. "I couldna get back when I wanted so I came here instead."

"Leaving a man to die!"

"No, I didna." He pointed at Jamie. "The lad's alive, and lookin' weel."

"But I'm not talking about Jamie, Cameron." Rory's voice went quiet, barely above a whisper. In the corner of his eye, he saw Jamie's expression change. The lad had already witnessed too much but Rory had to press his advantage.

"Who are ye talkin' about then, Ruairidh? I dinna hae the faintest idea." Auld Cameron sat up now, his back straight. His hands moved toward the hem of his kilt. He laid them flat on his thighs, apparently relaxed. Rory was not fooled.

"You tell me." Rory shifted his weight, propped up one knee and leaned on it with his elbow. "I never saw who it was but I'm fairly sure it was you who shot at me from the other cave a few nights ago."

Before Auld Cameron could move, Rory drew a pistol from inside his coat and aimed it at the drover's head. "The truth if you please. And hands up behind your head."

"Ruairidh, what—?"

"Hands up, Cameron! Jamie?" He nodded toward the lad. "Check for his pistol and take it. Then keep an eye out for company from the entrance. I don't trust this rat as far as I can spit."

"Aye, sir." Hands trembling, the lad removed Auld Cameron's pistol which he found tucked inside a bag sock, and took up station behind the crumbling wall near the door.

Rory kept his attention on the man opposite him. Sweat beaded Auld Cameron's wrinkled forehead; he waved his hands behind his head.

"The truth, Cameron." Rory cocked his pistol and aimed between the man's eyes. "Now."

"Ruairidh, I...I..." Terror grew in Auld Cameron's eyes as he stared past him.

Rory whirled round to the sound of a musket going off. He threw himself to the ground and rolled away into the shadows of a wall. Looking back, he watched Auld Cameron as he slumped, eyes wide open, a bright red hole gaping in the center of his chest.

Rory swore, glanced at Jamie, and was relieved to find the lad scurrying into the shadows. At least he was safe. The enemy must have snuck up on them from the back of the croft, hidden by darkness, where crumbling walls provided the perfect approach. Rory swore again. Whoever it was could have shot him first, sitting in front of the fire in full view. Why hadn't he?

Rory signaled to Jamie to stay down. He crawled toward the far corner where the shot came from, all the while keeping close to the wall. Sharp stones dug deep into his hands and shins, and he gritted his teeth. He crouched against the corner where the wall had collapsed. When he felt a mound of rubble, Rory carefully stepped onto it. It must be the same on the other side. The stones crunched underneath his boots, but he pulled himself along with his hands, climbing as high as he dared.

Whoever was on the other side probably heard him but he did not dare delay any longer. He took a deep breath and straightened, leaning over the wall with his toes barely reaching the top of the pile and his pistol pointed into the darkness. But the other side was empty. The attacker had fled in silence. Then the distant sound of hooves beating the ground reached him.

Damn it to bloody hell!

He scrambled down the gravel and ran to the entrance. Jamie stood, eyes wide. "They're gone, sir."

"Yes, I can see that." Rory took the pistol off the boy, secured it, and shoved it into his belt. He'd keep his own cocked a little while longer. He did not trust the silence.

"Let's move, lad. Quick. Before they come back." Rory strode toward the horses, his gaze roaming across the darkness. Yes, he'd heard a horse leave but were they really safe?

"Aye, sir." The lad jumped into his saddle, turning his mount to follow Rory's lead. "Where are we going?"

"To Inverness. I have to make sure we arrive before the attackers. Otherwise *we* might end up accused of murdering Auld Cameron. The whole affair smells of a trap."

"But it wasn't us, sir. Shouldn't we go after the murderers?"

Rory turned to look at the boy. His face was pale in the scant moonlight, and he was shaking. Damn, he should not have brought him. The lad was too green behind the ears.

"No point now, Jamie. Either they're safely away, or setting another trap. We can't risk it. Stay close behind me." He urged his horse to a canter along the gravel path that took them across the hills. One hand on the reins, he kept his pistol cocked, ready to shoot with no questions asked. Whoever shot Auld Cameron, must have valuable knowledge about Rory's business. He was still unsure if Auld Cameron tried to trap him—or if someone else was behind it all. Auld Cameron had been a crafty soul, but not the cleverest. No, this must be part of a wider plan.

The cave was no longer safe. No doubt, it would soon be swarmed with Redcoats. He hoped they would not spot the hidden entrance to the manor. If they did, it would take all his —and Auntie Meg's—powers of persuasion to deny any knowledge.

Teeth gritted, he urged his mount forward in the scarce moonlight peeking through the clouds.

***

The candle burned down another notch when Catriona finally put the book down and rose from the bed, her bare feet light on the floorboards. It must be after midnight. Despite the delightful company of Auntie Meg, the day dragged as they sat out of doors in the warm spring sunshine, adorning a quilt for a neighboring widow with a pattern of roses. Needlework was the bane of her life, each stitch after painstaking stitch sapping her concentration, but an afternoon nap helped revive her enough to stay awake late.

Only now, hours after the household retired, was it quiet enough for her mission. She picked up her slippers, took the candle, and, avoiding the creaky step, tiptoed down the stairs to the library. The door locked behind her, she dropped her slippers to the floor, sliding her feet into them. Tonight she'd find out what was hidden in the cave.

Catriona ducked underneath the lintel and pulled the lever. Even though she expected it, the sound of the stone wall grating still made her jump. In the silence of the night it sounded like an explosion ripping through the house.

Hovering in the opening, she listened for any signs of life. But all remained quiet. After releasing a long breath, she shuffled through the entrance into the tunnel and slid the door back into place. Goosebumps formed on her skin as the chilly, damp air hit her. She should have brought a wrap. Oh, silly—always forgetting something. Too late to go back; someone might hear her. Holding the flickering candle aloft, she slowly followed the tunnel.

Her progress was slow, as she stubbed her toes into many of the small outcrops of rock. Again, she marveled how Rory caught up with her so quickly the last time she'd been down here. He must know every twist and turn like the back of his hand. As she thought of him, a sense of foreboding twisted her gut, a faint feeling he might be in peril. Her heart contracted.

Nonsense! She shrugged off the dark thoughts. It was just the confined space, and the atmosphere of danger down here making her worry.

He was able to look after himself. Auntie Meg said so.

Catriona edged forward until she came to the spot where the tunnel forked. Again, she took the right turn, narrower and darker than before—if that was even possible. She shuffled forward. The candle burned another half notch. Had she been here for half an hour already?

Finally, in the distance, she saw a light. She wanted to slump against the wall in relief. But only a moment later she tensed again, because what on earth was a light doing in the cave this late at night?

Near the exit, brightly illuminated now she was so close, she halted. Feeling around, she found a small ledge, dribbled a few drops of wax onto it, and secured the candle into place. With her hands against the rough surface, she stepped toward the gap in the wall. Muffled voices reached her. Men shouting. Why were they in the cave at this late hour? Was Rory amongst them? She took a deep breath and, holding it, nudged toward the edge, and peeked around. The light came from another cave behind the empty one she faced. Not trusting the voices, Lowland Scots and English accents alike, she stayed hidden behind the rock, trying to hear what was being said. Only snippets filtered through to her. Catriona froze.

Muskets. Rebellion. Cameron. Trap. A dead man.

Chapter Eleven

Oh, Rory! Her heart skipped a beat, and she balled her hands into fists to stop them from shaking as she leaned back against the wall. They must be talking about Rory. Was he the dead man? Or the killer? With a start, she remembered the shot she heard when she was last down here. Had he shot someone? A smuggler? Or a government agent?

The voices grew faint. Releasing her breath, she peeked around the edge again. In the other cave she saw shadows of men moving around, as if looking for something. Muskets? A flash of red jacket caught her eye.

Redcoats.

The government troops must have discovered the cave and suspected the worst. She bit her lip, praying Rory did not venture out on the loch tonight. Not knowing where he was —and whether he was safe—was tearing her apart. She must warn him. But what if he came to the cave before going home? He'd walk right into a trap.

He'd hang.

Her whole body shook with horror as she realized Rory's business activities were far more dangerous than she'd thought. Yes, he was a Jacobite, but he was more involved than that. He smuggled arms. The soldiers spoke of crates full of muskets. Someone betrayed him—that much was certain. His life was in danger.

Determined to find him before the Redcoats did, she turned back into the tunnel. Someone knew where he was. Catriona picked up her candle, ignoring the dust that floated off the ledge and lifted her skirts with her other hand. She'd taken but a few steps when her nose itched. Dropping her skirts, she covered it with her arm, not daring to breathe. Please, God, not here. Not now.

The sneeze shook her as she tried in vain to muffle any sounds with her elbow. Hot wax covered her hand and she winced. Hearing raised voices in the cave, she charged forward. Again. Just like the last time, except now it was not Rory chasing after her. It was the Law. She had given away the secret. Blast! They would search for the tunnel entrance, and they were bound to find it.

Tears filled her eyes, blurring her vision. Oh, what had she done! Catriona took no regard of her dress snagging on outcropping rock, her feet in agony from stumbling over sharp stones. She did not dare stop to look behind her but the sound of voices carried through the tunnel.

They found it.

The voices became louder, getting closer. At the fork, she stopped to the sound of heavy footsteps.

I must guide them away from the house.

Without hesitation, she veered into the other path, praying it provided her with a safe exit.

She didn't know where this path ended. It was wider, and more level. Perhaps it led to another cave on the shore. She prayed the Redcoats had not yet discovered it. With large steps, she plunged into the darkness, her candle providing only little comfort now she had to shield it with her hand to keep the small flame alight. The men's voices were still faint, yet they kept up with her. She broke into a run, hoping to gain some time. A few turns onwards, she bumped into a wall.

A dead end.

No! There must be a door, like the one in the library. She scraped her fingers along the walls around her but did not find a lever. Not even a gap in the stonework.

Terrified, she lifted her candle and took a step back. A solid wall with nowhere to go. Her heart raced, each beat pounding in her ears.

What would they do if they caught up with her? Torture her to reveal Rory's secrets? Kill her? Down here, she'd never be found, her life worthless. They'd get away with murder and Rory'd be left to live with it. He'd warned her of the danger she might find herself in yet she refused to listen. Now his words had become terrifying reality. An icy shiver ran down her spine.

Deep breaths. Catriona forced herself to calm, her shallow breathing still betraying her fears.

Then she heard it, faint and barely audible. A whining sound. Behind the wall. She stared at the stone in front of her where the sound seemed to come from. High pitched, like an animal.

A seal?

Goosebumps covered her skin as she slid her hand over the wall again, slower this time. Crouching, she spotted a narrow gap. Her fingers just about managed to slip underneath, and she nearly screamed when they closed around a narrow lever. She pulled it to either side but nothing happened. Lights were dancing at the far end of the tunnel. The voices were now clearer, footsteps echoing louder. They were close. Too close.

In desperation she pushed the lever, and fell over when the wall slid upwards. It stopped barely four feet off the ground. Without hesitation, she shuffled on all fours through the gap. Her hand found the lever, and she pushed it back into place just as the light of a torch hit the wall opposite.

Leaning against the stone, Catriona caught her breath. She heard the faint sound of footsteps, and voices, and prayed they didn't find the lever.

Calm, she needed to calm down. And keep moving. The whining stopped the moment she pushed the lever. Thank God. As if the sound also did not wish to help the soldiers. A shiver trickled down her spine.

Getting to her feet, she lifted the candle and looked around. The sight that greeted her took her breath away. A strange light shimmered high above her but it was not daylight. Long spikes hung from the ceiling, with moisture dripping to the ground, forming small pillars that rose from the ground. She carefully walked toward one and touched it.

It felt wet, yet smooth, as if the dripping never stopped.

Awed by such a glorious display, she looked around the cave. This was most unusual. Never had she seen such beauty as the sparkling ceiling, and the sea of pillars and spikes. On the far side, the cave narrowed into another tunnel. A trickle of water ran through it, forming a pool in the center of the cave. It was magical. Catriona walked toward the water's edge and dunked her hand into it. The chill made her shiver, yet felt refreshing at the same time. She saw no sign of any living thing, seal or otherwise. How very strange!

When faint banging ripped through the silence, her gaze fell toward the spot where she'd entered, and she straightened. The men might still discover the exit. With a final glance at the shimmering display, she followed the stream, keeping to the path next to it. With a little luck, she'd find the way out. The rock was slippery in places, and she was forced to catch her balance more often than not, scraping her hands, and soaking her feet. The faint light seemed to linger all along this tunnel, providing her with just enough vision. Her candle burned another notch. She had little time left. Around her, the rocks were closing, forming another tunnel with the water streaming through the center.

As the candle neared the lowest notch, barely above her fingers, Catriona saw a light in the distance. The exit? With a sigh of relief, she hurried toward it, sliding on the uneven ground. Hot wax dripped onto her skin, and she blew out the candle and left it on a ledge. It was now light enough without it. The water flowed stronger, as if fed by a current, and as the gap grew narrower, she had to crouch. Her eyes slowly adjusted to the brighter light. It must be dawn by now.

Emerging from the tunnel, she lifted her hand against the glare. Carefully looking around, she inched outside, pushing thorny brambles out of the way. No ships in sight anywhere.

The entrance was level with the loch, but the thicket of brambles hid it from view. The gap was too small for a boat, too small even to shift crates, so no good for smuggling. But it formed the perfect escape route for a person. Thank goodness!

Catriona picked up her soaked slippers and gasped when her feet hit the cold water, but she saw no other way back to firm ground. She scrambled along on slippery rocks, for if anyone were to spot her now, they'd know where to find the entrance. The sun was rising behind her, bathing the opposite shore in golden light. Hopefully anyone looking her way from the other side would be blinded by its brightness. She sent a little prayer heavenward. Finally, her hands and legs wet and scratched, she spotted the boathouse. Hurrying now, she finally slid inside and leaned against the wall, catching her breath. But she must not linger. Time was of the essence.

She had to find Rory.

***

Rory kept his head low as he skirted the steep walls of Inverness Castle, with his collar pulled up high. A glance over his shoulder showed him Jamie followed suit. British government soldiers patrolled the grounds, and he could not risk attracting unwanted attention.

It took them several days of barely interrupted travel. No rest for the horses, nor themselves. Little sleep in damp forests made them grumpy.

With Jamie right behind him, he dived back into the narrow lanes, away from the river Ness, and stopped outside a tavern. One look through the open, grime-stained door was enough to make a hardened man flinch but he still burst out laughing at Jamie's horrified expression.

"Stay close to me, lad." Rory slapped Jamie on the shoulder and entered, ducking underneath the low frame. The boy did as he was bid. Good!

"No worries, lad," he whispered. "This place looks worse than it is." He gestured to a vacant table. "Let's settle in that corner."

Pulling his coat open, he grabbed a rickety chair and settled onto it, gesturing to the serving wench for a jug of ale.

He frowned as he watched the boy gingerly sit on a stool, his back firmly against the solid wall, wide eyes scanning the room.

"Here ye are, sir," the wench greeted him as she bent over to put two tankards and a pitcher filled with frothy ale onto their table. Her hand still resting on the handle, she wriggled as if her gown was suddenly too tight, and Rory found himself confronted by a pair of large, bouncy breasts straining to be freed from their prison. "Anythin' else I can get ye?" Her smile was suggestive, although her yellow teeth somewhat dented the appeal.

Rory smiled and squeezed some coins into her hand. "No thanks, lass. We're here to talk, not to dally in other hazards." He winked as her smile grew wider at the sight of his generous offer. Quickly, she stuffed the coins into the pouch at her belt.

"Shame, sir," she whispered, her gaze raking over his frame. "But as ye wish." With a flourish, she turned and sauntered back to the bar, hips swaying with each step.

Rory chuckled but grew sober when he felt Jamie's gaze on him. The lad's face was puce. Rory poured ale into their tankards and picked his up. "Drink, lad. We might have to wait a while, so you might make the most of it." He took a deep draught and watched as Jamie took his tankard, sipping slowly. "They don't poison you here. It may look like a hovel..." His gaze wandered around the soot-covered walls and grimy tables. "But it's the ideal meeting place. Trust me."

"I do, sir." Jamie's voice shook. "I really do. But I've...I've never been in such a tavern before."

Rory nodded, aware of the lad's rural upbringing. It seemed Robbie MacKinnon had not bothered to introduce his son to the vices of the world yet. Well, this visit to Inverness went some way toward rectifying his lack of worldliness. Given Jamie's reaction to the serving wench's ample offerings, clearly lasses were another pleasure the lad had not yet experienced. He wondered how far he had gone with Mairi. The maid seemed so much more mature than Jamie, yet a spark had kindled between them.

His smile faded when he remembered another spark, much

closer to home. Closer to his heart. Nay, not his heart, but his loins. No woman would ever claim ownership of his heart. He did not allow for such frivolity. His allegiance to the Stuart cause too much a risk to burden a woman with. Soon they would rebel again, no doubt. And as before, widows and orphans were always left behind to deal with life's hardships.

Rory hated being the bearer of bad news in the wake of the last rebellion, and the pain he'd seen in the faces of his clansmen's widows cured him of ever wanting to love a woman that much, or be loved in return. Yes, one day he was going to wed—especially if he inherited Auntie Meg's lands—but without any feelings involved. So nobody would mourn for him should he be killed in battle; no heartbroken widow left to cry over his dead body. 'Twas better that way.

He emptied his tankard with a large draught and refilled it. Holding it between both hands, he watched the serving wench as she hopped onto another punter's lap, her plump curves bouncing. The memory of Catriona's curves shivering beneath his hands came without warning. Rory closed his eyes, willing the image to disappear. Yet before him, he saw her lying in the middle of the boat, lips apart, waiting for his kiss, her nipples tightening under his tongue. Her long tresses spread out over the planks. The lass was everything a man needed. Everything a man wanted.

When he felt the stirrings of desire in his loins, he crossed his legs. He'd not taken her that day, but take her he would. Every fiber of him wanted to ravish her, to make her his.

Just for one night.

That was, if she had not fled back to Edinburgh yet. In that case, he would be glad to be rid of her. She stirred more than just feelings of desire. Catriona was so fragile, making him want to protect her—to look after her. And he could not allow that.

He set down the tankard with a thud and cursed. "Where is he?" he muttered, more to himself than Jamie.

"Who are we waiting for, sir?" the lad piped up, an empty pitcher in front of him and the hint of a smile on his face. My, the lad was getting drunk fast. Rory refilled their tankards and grinned. Oh, to be so young again. So innocent.

"It's an old friend of mine, lad. He's got information." He sipped at the frothy liquid. The ale in this tavern was of better quality than the premises themselves. Another advantage.

"Information about what?" Jamie stared at him.

Rory leaned over, his voice low. "About our friend at the croft."

Jamie's eyes widened. "The de—"

"Here's Malcolm." Rory cast the lad a warning glance as he waived to the man entering the tavern. He grinned as Jamie's jaw dropped.

Rory stood and greeted the soldier, their hands meeting in a firm grasp. "Good to see you, Malcolm Campbell."

"Aye, Rory Cameron, it's been a long while." His eyes twinkled when his gaze fell onto Jamie. "And who's your companion?"

"Malcolm, this is Jamie MacKinnon, Robbie's lad." Rory turned to the boy who stood gaping at the new arrival. He should have warned him their informant was a soldier for the British Crown. He laid his hand on the lad's shoulder and pulled him back to his seat. "Jamie, may I present Major Malcolm Campbell."

"A Redcoat?" Accusation glittered in Jamie's eyes, and his voice shook. But he followed Rory's lead and sat.

Malcolm chuckled. "My, he's quick." He gestured to the wench for more ale.

Rory nodded. "He's young. He'll learn." He glanced at the boy. Jamie emptied his tankard. "Steady, lad. We need to keep a clear head." He waited while the serving maid brought another jug and tankard, then turned to his old friend.

"What's the word out there, Malcolm?"

The other man's rugged face grew serious. "I don't know what happened but word is that you killed a government agent."

"A what?" Rory swore. "The dead man was no agent—he was a two-faced drover who tried his luck with me one time too many. I was just about to get the story from him. The murderer escaped clean." He mulled over it for a moment.

"Now I can see why. Much easier to blame the murder on someone else, and pretend Auld Cameron was an agent. Well, maybe he was. A double-dealing agent."

"Damn. You didn't recognize the killer?"

Rory shook his head. "No. The shot came from behind me. Jamie here was guarding the entrance to the croft but the bastard scaled the wall of a far corner. Neither of us saw him. By the time we turned, he'd gone." He emptied his tankard and set it down. "And now I'm being framed for it."

"Aye, it seems so." Malcolm looked from him to the lad. "You didn't see any movement outside the croft, Jamie?"

"No, sir. All was still outside the entrance." He glanced at Rory who nodded in encouragement. "After the shot, we heard a horse in a copse round the back, and someone sliding down the rubble. I...I was surprised the killer didn't shoot us, too. I still don't understand." His gaze darted between the two men.

"So they can blame it on Rory here. And you by association, although your name hasn't been mentioned."

"That's a relief," Rory muttered. "As long as it's only my head on the block, I'm content."

"Stop fooling yourself, Rory," Malcolm growled. "I don't want to see you paying the price for someone else's foul deed. But what I haven't told you yet is that I have a lead already. The trail goes all the way to Edinburgh."

"Edinburgh?" Rory echoed. "Someone in high places?"

"Worse, someone with money problems." Malcolm's face looked grim.

Rory leaned back. That explained a lot. He let out a slow whistle. "An investor?"

Malcolm's eyes twinkled. "You're as quick as your reputation promises. Aye, someone who's lost money thanks to some of your, erm, transactions." He leaned forward and whispered, "Someone who expected a delivery of muskets."

Jamie's eyes widened and he opened his mouth. Rory slapped the lad's back, and he burst into a coughing fit. "Steady, Jamie! Have another sip of ale." He refilled the boy's tankard and pushed it into his hands.

"I see." A smile played around Rory's lips.

Over the last few months, he heard reports of an Edinburgh banker keen to get his hands on the muskets he'd hidden after the previous year's failed uprising. Rory had been part of a group of Jacobites who secreted away the crates from Glen Shiel. But when rumor became rife that someone was keen to buy them, it caused a quarrel between the smugglers.

One side—Rory's side—wanted to keep them safe for future use, a new rebellion. The other party wanted to make a quick profit, regarding it as too dangerous a cargo to hang on to. Auld Cameron had been their vocal leader.

Without telling his associates, Rory had moved the guns to a secure location with the help of a small handful of friends. But he knew it was only a matter of time until his associates returned with questions. Clearly, in light of the murder, they were done waiting for answers.

"Why don't you give them what they want?" Malcolm's eyes bore hints of concern. "That may stifle the rumors and the fuss might die down."

"You know as well as I do that wouldn't happen, even if I did give them the location, which I never will," he added with emphasis. "Has a warrant been issued yet?"

Malcolm shook his head. "Not yet. But someone has friends in high places. It won't take long for them to appear on your doorstep."

"You mean Aunt Meg's doorstep?"

"Aye. As the estate is your inheritance anyway. They'll use this unsavory incident to get rid of you for good and open up good land to the competition."

Rory's head was spinning. The situation was worse than he expected. Attacking him was one thing—he'd deal with any threat. But if someone dared threaten Auntie Meg, or Catriona, they'd pay with their lives. "Thanks, Malcolm. I appreciate your help."

He emptied the dregs from his tankard and stood. Jamie jumped up, toppling over his stool. Blushing, he righted it. Rory held his hand out to Malcolm, and the two men took their leave.

"Farewell, my friend."

"Farewell, Rory. Watch yourself!" Malcolm's troubled expression did not lighten when Rory patted his back.

"Don't fret. I'll find a way out of this mess." With a final nod, he added, "I'll be in touch." He pulled his collar up again, casting most of his face into shadow.

"Godspeed," Malcolm said, his eyes morose.

Rory shook off the overpowering feeling of dread and pushed Jamie toward the door. "Let's go. We have to get back."

Outside the entrance, Jamie stopped short. "But, sir, we've only just arrived."

Rory nodded. "I know, lad. I'm tired, too, but we have to get out of the city." He scanned the narrow streets. "Too many ears."

"Ah." Jamie followed him down the lane toward the blacksmith where they'd stabled their horses. "But can we stop for food?"

"Aye." Rory laughed. "See the pie seller on the corner? Let's get some provisions for our journey."

Chapter Twelve

Catriona burst through the kitchen door and collapsed onto the floor, her breathing ragged, and her heartbeat pounding in her ears. Mairi rushed to her side, wiping her hands on her apron. Supporting Catriona's back, the maid leaned her against a chest by the window. The need for oblivion kept Catriona's eyelids closed but she felt Mairi's hands on her forehead and neck, checking temperature and pulse.

"What on earth's happened to you? Stay with me."

Catriona blinked and finally pried her eyes open, gazing into nowhere. It took a few moments for her to focus on her surroundings. She watched as Mairi rose, grabbed a jug, and dashed outside. Liquid splashed into the copper container. The maid returned, picked a bowl from a shelf, and poured water into it. From a basket, she took a clean rag, dipped it into the water, and kneeling by her side, dabbed Catriona's forehead.

The cool liquid ran down her burning cheeks, dripping into her cleavage. It tickled but the shock sensation revived her senses. Mairi wrung out the cloth, dipped, and applied it again. Catriona's heartbeat began to ease.

"Rory," she croaked.

"Rory? What about him? Has he returned?" The maid's eyes lit before wariness replaced the shine. She frowned. "Rory's not responsible for the state of you, is he?"

Catriona shook her head and Mairi released a slow breath.

"No, I have to warn him." Catriona forced herself into a more upright position but still didn't dare get on her feet. She was still quite shaken. "Redcoats."

Mairi stood and glanced out of the window. "Redcoats? Here?"

"Soon. They'll be here soon. They found the cave." The adrenaline was wearing off and Catriona wanted to melt into a puddle on the floor. She wanted to hide under her covers and sleep for days. But now was not the time for rest. "I have to warn Rory. If he goes to the cave, they..." Her voice trailed off.

Mairi eyed her suspiciously. "How do you know about the cave?" She took a cup and filled it with fresh water from the jug. Holding it out to Catriona, she added, "They won't be able to take action against him. The crates are gone."

Catriona held the cup with both hands and gulped the water, washing away the dust from the tunnels and wetting her parched throat. "I heard a shot in the tunnel a few nights ago. Someone's been killed and Rory knows." Staring at Mairi, who had become more sister than servant, she whispered, "He was in the cave when I heard the shot."

She pushed herself up to sit on the chest, leaning her back against the windowsill. Holding out her cup, she waited until Mairi refilled it and then emptied it again in one draught. Suspicion flashed in the girl's eyes, and something else. Surprise?

"How did you know about the tunnel?"

"I spotted Rory coming out of the library late one night." Her cheeks began to burn at the memory. "I was curious so I went to see for myself. The night of the shot, after I'd run back through the tunnel to the house, Rory was just behind me. He brought Jamie with him."

Relieved to share her burden, she leaned her head back against the windowpane and closed her eyes. Just for a moment.

"Jamie was there, too?"

Catriona heard a chair creak. "Yes," she confirmed. "He looked scared." She opened her eyes to the distant sound of horses' hooves. "Oh my God, is that them?"

Mairi stood and raced toward the open door. Glancing out, she shouted at Catriona. "Aye, a small group of Redcoats are coming from the direction of the cave. Go upstairs and change dress. They mustn't see you all soaked and muddy."

She rushed back inside, straight into the pantry. "Time to prepare luncheon to make it look inconspicuous."

Catriona heaved herself from the chest. By the kitchen door, she halted and turned. "What about Auntie Meg?"

"Don't worry about Lady Meg, Catriona. She's been dealing with them for too many decades for us to ever worry." The maid winked at her. "And she knows naught of importance so she can't be caught lying. Now away with ye!"

Catriona pounded up the stairs, her skirt hitched high for her to take two steps at a time. Changing fast was difficult but she forced herself to get through this. For Auntie Meg. For Rory. They'd given her a home. She was not going to let them down. When she peeled off her soaked gown, voices reached her from the yard.

Gathering the dirty mess, she pushed it to the bottom of her clothes chest, threw her grimy slippers and stockings after it, and took a plain linen dress from the top. Quickly she pulled it on, fastening the laces as best as she managed without help, and slid into fresh stockings.

Picking a sturdy pair of shoes, she put them on and cast a glance into the mirror. Solid, earthy. She'd fit right in here. Her hair was a mess, long strands tumbling down her neck. She gathered it and tied it into a bun at her nape, securing the stubborn tresses with several long pins.

Finished!

Descending the stairs, she prayed the Redcoats would not see through her lies. She'd never been comfortable lying—that was Angus' forte—but if she had to she could. She stopped halfway when the naked truth hit her. She'd do anything for Rory. He'd taken her heart. It no longer was hers alone.

Her need to protect him, to save him from harm, was essential. She'd protect him at the risk of her own safety. This knowledge came as a shock, but nevertheless was true. Forcing a calm she didn't feel, she continued down the stairs.

The voices came from the drawing room. Thank God Mairi kept them from the library. Catriona wondered how the girl had become so clever, so mischievous.

Was she really only a maid?

She shook her head to rid herself from any traitorous thoughts. When she entered the room, the conversation stilled.

"We have guests, Mairi? I thought I heard voices."

"Yes, Miss Catriona. This gentleman here is Major Robertson." She pointed at a man standing by the window, dressed in a vibrant red coat and pantaloons with not a crease in sight. "Major, this is Miss Catriona MacKenzie, Lady Margaret's goddaughter from Edinburgh. She's here to recuperate from a recent illness." Mairi's gaze bored into her.

Catriona smiled at the major and, gesturing him toward the armchair, sat on the sofa. "Major Robertson, will you please take a seat? I must apologize at my rudeness in sitting. I'm still feeling a little bit faint." At least that wasn't a lie. The major obliged and, with a little bow, seated himself on the edge of the chair.

"Mairi, please inform Lady Margaret of our guest. And bring refreshments." Dismissing the maid with a nod, she watched the soldier carefully. "What brings you here, Major Robertson?"

"Miss MacKenzie, I'm here on a delicate issue." He hesitated, his gaze taking in her plain appearance. Good, all going to plan. "Whatever it was you were suffering of, I pray your recovery is proceeding well?" The Lowland accent was crisp, almost indistinguishable.

"It is indeed. I have begun to feel most refreshed. The air in Edinburgh is ghastly, especially as the temperature rises this time of year." She shook her head. "No cure works better than taking fresh Highland air." His eyebrows shot up. Clearly, the major did not agree with her.

"But you're not here to enquire about my health." She cast him a sweet smile, inwardly wondering what Mairi told Auntie Meg.

"Indeed, Miss MacKenzie, indeed. I'm here on an altogether more unsavory duty." His gaze locked with hers. "We're looking for Rory Cameron, your godmother's nephew. Have you met him?"

"I have met Mr Cameron, but only briefly. He never stays for long." God, she hoped Auntie Meg would not tell him any differently. With a smile she hoped did not look as insincere as her thoughts, she prodded for information. "Why are you looking for him?"

Still focusing on her face, he said, "I'm afraid I have to arrest him."

Catriona gasped, her hands flying to cover her cheeks. "Arrest Mr Cameron? But why? Surely this must be a mistake." Her pulse beat violently at her neck, and she stifled the impulse to cover it.

"I can assure you that this is no misunderstanding. Mr Cameron shot a man in cold blood. There were witnesses."

Catriona's eyes widened. Had they caught Jamie, perhaps even tortured him?

"Witnesses?" She rose and walked to the window, barely aware the major jumped to his feet. He had the manners of a man of good breeding. Dull, and oh so predictable. "My, this will inconvenience Lady Margaret most awfully, Major Robertson. You see, she is such a gentle lady." She turned to face him, her gaze imploring.

The major coughed. "I'm terribly sorry, Miss, but I have to know when you last saw Mr Cameron."

Catriona's mind was spinning. Dear God, how could she save Rory if there were witnesses? "Several days ago I saw him last. Four, I believe. Or three? Dearie me, I'm not certain." She let out a giggle, and a silent prayer he'd believe her to be a simple girl.

Auntie Meg took this moment to enter, her walking stick firmly in hand. "Good day, Major Robertson."

"Good day, Lady Margaret. I hope you're well."

A cold fear settled in Catriona's heart. They knew each other! She prayed she'd not revealed too much.

Auntie Meg smiled at Catriona. "Major Robertson and I are old friends, aren't we?" She sent him a challenging look.

The wily old lady seemed to know exactly how to treat this particular visitor. Catriona held back a sigh of relief.

"I'm glad to hear, Auntie Meg. Will you take a seat?" She

guided Auntie Meg to the settee and helped her settle into it before joining her.

"Thank you, dear. Major, please." The soldier did as he was bid, crouching into the armchair again.

Catriona nodded at her godmother. "The major was just about to tell me what happened. Rory is in ghastly trouble."

"Is he now?" The old lady winked at the major. "When isn't he, then?"

Mairi entered with a tray laden with a teapot, china cups, and a plate of oatcakes. She poured each a cup before, with a curtsy, she excused herself, leaving the door ajar.

The major waited until the door closed, then put his cup on the table. He leaned forward, hands folded on his knees. "I'm afraid, Lady Margaret, that the matter is more serious than Mr Cameron's usual misdemeanors."

Holy Christ, he knew of the smuggling. Catriona's cup rattled on the saucer. "Oh, it's hot," she mumbled and set the delicate china onto the tray. "I do apologize. Pray continue."

"Yes, what's the boy up to now?" Auntie Meg watched him over the rim of her cup.

"I'm sorry to cause you such anxiety, Lady Margaret. This time it's very serious. Mr Cameron murdered a government agent and left the body to rot in the hills just south of Inverness."

Auntie Meg's cup and saucer dropped to the floor too fast for Catriona to catch them, spilling tea over the rug. Her godmother's face went white, and she leaned back, gasping for air. Catriona ignored the major and popped open a button at the old lady's throat. Auntie Meg's breathing steadied yet her eyes remained closed. Catriona squeezed her hand and looked back at the soldier.

"As you see, Major Robertson, this has come as quite a shock. Lady Margaret needs rest." She stood, squaring up to him. "I'd appreciate it if you brought proof of your accusation next time you grace us with your company. For now, I bid you farewell. I have to look after my godmother."

He took a step toward her and grabbed her arm. Long fingers dug deep into her flesh. She winced.

"And I, Miss MacKenzie, don't like being taken for a fool. Where is Cameron?"

She tugged her arm but could not shake his hand off. Worry about her godmother mingled with fear for Rory's life. "I don't know. I really don't. He left without a word." The soldier pushed her away and marched to the door. Holding it open, he turned.

"I hope for your—and the old lady's— sake that you're telling the truth. I'd not wish to take her lands, but if she's found harboring a suspected murderer that's exactly what I'm going to do. Now, I'm to find Cameron. And don't be fooled into doing anything stupid, Miss MacKenzie. We're watching you. Closely." He slammed the door behind him.

Catriona sank onto the settee, grabbing Auntie Meg's hand. "Auntie?" She fanned her other hand in front of the pale face. Her godmother's eyes flew open.

"Is he gone?" she whispered.

Catriona nodded, relief flooding through her, as Auntie Meg seemed to experience the most miraculous recovery. "Yes, I believe so." Letting herself fall against the hard back of the settee, she shook her head. "What are we going to do?"

"I tell you what we're going to do, dear." Auntie Meg sat up, took Catriona's cup from the tray, and emptied it in a few fast gulps. "That's better. Now, do you have any idea where Rory might be?"

Catriona shook her head. "No. He didn't talk to me after..." She blushed. "But, dear Lord, the gunshots." She stared at Auntie Meg whose brows shot up.

"Gunshots?"

"The major said that the body was near Inverness."

Her godmother nodded.

"Now, why would he take a body all the way from the cave to Inverness?"

"A body? In the cave?" A set of sharp blue eyes bore into her. "How do you know about the cave?"

"It's a long story. But I heard a shot in the cave one night when I explored the tunnel. And then Rory came back with Jamie MacKinnon." Her mind went back to that night. "It can't be the same body. That means he's killed twice." A sob escaped her lips.

"Nonsense!" Auntie Meg's voice cut through her anguish. "Rory never killed anyone. It's obvious he's being framed. I'd just like to know by whom." She reached out and refilled their cups, having picked up hers from the floor. She thrust one into Catriona's hands. "Drink up! And then we have to make plans." She leaned back, a pensive look in her eyes, sipping at the stale liquid.

Catriona watched her, wondering not for the first time whether her godmother was made of sterner stuff than she led people to believe. She'd feigned her collapse most believably. Looking at her now, hands calm, drinking tea, Catriona was certain the old lady was craftier than she thought.

Mairi came in, closing the door behind her, and leaned against it. "They're gone."

"Good. Then let's think. Where could Rory be headed for?" Auntie Meg stared at the dregs in her cup, as if to find the answer.

"The gallows if it's up to the major," Mairi growled.

"Don't say that." Catriona shivered. Ignoring the speculative glance the maid cast her she refilled her cup, and drained it in one draught. "Does he know anyone in Inverness?"

Her godmother laughed. "Aye, he knows half the city while the other half wants his head. But given that's near where the body was found, we can assume he went there. So he has to come down the route along the glens."

Mairi nodded. "Aye, shall we send someone to look for him?"

"That's a good idea, Mairi. Send that young lad of Ewan Cameron's. He did well enough last time. But wait till after nightfall."

Mairi agreed. "Aye, too many Redcoats swarming around. Don't worry, Catriona. We'll find him, and we'll warn him." She lifted the tray and left.

"But Auntie Meg, he's been accused of murder. Surely, he

can't come back to the house."

"That's true, dearie. But Rory's been set up before and he's always found a way out of it. He'll know what to do."

"I'm worried. Two dead men. How can he possibly wriggle out of that?"

Her godmother laughed. "One body. Two bodies. Rory's escaped the noose more often than you can imagine, lass. All we need to do is warn him to be on his guard. Young Ewan will find him. I've no doubt."

Catriona nodded. "If you say so." She sat up. "I hate waiting. I want to do something."

"Ach, I know. The waiting game is a woman's fate. We wait to grow up, wait for our prince, all the while hoping we don't end up married off to an ogre. Then we wait for our husbands to return unscathed from battle."

Sadness filled her eyes and Catriona clasped her hand. Her godmother's gaze met hers. "Your Uncle Alan was a fine man. An honest and fair man. And here I am, old and frail, still waiting for him to come back to me. But he never will. That long-ago night in Glencoe, at the chieftain's house, he learnt the lesson of trust deceived the hard way and paid for it with his life. I've waited long enough. Soon it'll be my time to join him. Then I won't have to wait anymore." Tears rolled down the wrinkled cheeks.

Catriona dabbed her godmother's face with a kerchief. "Not yet, Auntie Meg. You've still much to do here. Like looking after Rory. Uncle Alan will have to wait a little longer." The old lady smiled, her hand stroking Catriona's. "If I had a daughter, I wish she'd be like you. She'd look after Rory."

Chapter Thirteen

Rory stretched out flat on his stomach behind the brambles by the roadside, keeping his face low. The grass tickled his nose, and he quickly pinched it. Hopefully, his drab cloak provided him with the camouflage he needed, blending him into the muddy landscape.

Jamie stayed with the horses, hidden from sight behind a mound. But Rory needed to watch the soldiers. Heart pounding in his ears, he watched as the men marched in line up the narrow road toward Inverness, only yards from his hiding place. Pinched faces, shoulders hunched against the wind, they walked at a brisk pace.

Counting the rows passing by, he guessed there must be at least one hundred foot soldiers. Fortunately, their superiors rode ahead. He shuddered. If he'd not heard the hooves beating on the gravel, he'd have found himself in Inverness gaol, no doubt.

Rory decided to stay down until the last row turned a sharp bend ahead. It seemed like an eternity before he dared raise his head, scanning the roads and hillsides around him. Not a soul in sight. Relief washed over him when he thought how close he'd come to having himself arrested. It was time to leave the main roads and cut through the hills. He rose and hurried across the mound to where Jamie patiently waited with the horses.

"I think we're safe now." Rory shook the dust from his clothes. Taking the reins from Jamie, he heaved himself into the saddle. He grabbed the water skin, took a large draught, and passed it on to the boy.

"We head up on that hill." He pointed toward a peak behind them. "The road is too dangerous. I wonder how many more soldiers will be heading north." His mood was grim. "Watch your horse, lad. The ground is quite loose here."

"Aye, sir." Jamie's voice shook. "What would they've done with us if they caught us?"

"Thrown us into gaol, lad. Or thrown a noose over that tree ahead and done away with us. Who knows."

"W-without a trial?"

"Aye, without a trial. It's what happens in times of war."

"But, we're not at war now."

Rory turned to face him. "As long as we're ruled from London, we're always at war." He swore, dragging his hand through his hair. Deep breath. "Look, I'm sorry, lad. I'm angry, that's all. But not with you. Best leave me be a wee while, aye?"

Jamie nodded. "Aye, sir."

"Good. Then let's move on. The sooner we reach Loch Linnhe the better." He turned and began the climb the hill. The rabbit path was barely trod, but Rory knew all the hidden trails that cut across the Highland hills. He'd walked them plenty of times.

***

The sun was sinking low over the hills on the far shore when Rory stopped short. It took them five long days to reach the hamlet of Inverlochy. Several times they'd been forced to hide, once for almost half a day, when soldiers on patrol roamed the area. Patience was not his forte, and Rory was at boiling point. His skin was filthy, his clothes ragged and muddy. So many Redcoats. This was more than a simple manhunt. Were they searching for the muskets?

Of course. Rory raised his head as he stopped in the shadow of Inverlochy Castle. His hood low over his brow, he gestured Jamie to follow him in silence. The arms. How could he have forgotten about the muskets? Some military bigwig knew they were hidden in the Highlands. He thought of the cave, cut deep into the mountains, where the guns waited for him.

Ready for the next rebellion—*not* for one damned banker who'd sell them to the highest bidder—making a profit on the backs of honest Highland folk. He was never going to reveal the hiding place, not even to Jamie. He didn't dare put the boy's life in danger.

With grim resolve he rode on. They had barely reached the shore when a shadow darted from behind shrubs. "Mr Rory, Mr Rory."

Rory reined in his horse before it trampled over the boy jumping up and down in front of him. The lad was no older than 10 years. "Young Ewan."

"Mr Rory, quick. Awa' from the shore." A small finger pointed toward a frigatte far out on the water. "Come wi' me."

More Redcoats. Rory swore. Surely something else was afoot. He heaved himself off his horse and followed the boy as he darted between several hovels. Jamie followed his lead unasked. Once out of sight of the water, Young Ewan came to a halt.

"Mr Rory, Lady Meg sends me. The soldiers, they're looking for you."

Jamie took the reins off him and stayed behind, casting furtive glances toward the road.

Rory grabbed the boy's shoulder. "How long have you been waiting for me?"

"Seven days. The soldiers found your cave."

"Damn!" He nodded. "But at least they didn't find anything inside."

"No, but they found the tunnel. Mairi says they followed Miss Catriona to the other cave, the one where the black seal lives, but didn't find the entrance once the lady went through." The lad squirmed under Rory's glare. "I dinna ken who Miss Catriona is. But Mairi says they're safe for the moment. Miss Catriona and Lady Meg got rid of the soldiers."

"Thank you, Ewan. You staying with family?"

The boy gave him a crooked grin. "Aye, wi' ma sister. She

lives just here." He pointed at a small cottage with gaping holes for windows. The walls were whitewashed with lime some time ago but now it was covered in mud. Life was tough out here for ordinary folk.

The news was worse than expected, with the cave and tunnel exposed. Mairi was always careful to warn him of any goings-on. He pulled out a couple of coins and gave them to the boy. "Be careful as always with them, Young Ewan. Don't want to attract undue attention."

Ewan's grin widened. "Nay, Mr Rory. Ye can count on me. They'll go in a safe place."

Rory nodded and thanked him. He watched the lad run to his sister's hut, closing the rickety door firmly behind him.

Jamie stared at him. "The safe place?"

Rory chuckled. "Aye. He's got a small box buried in the garden somewhere. Not sure if at his parents' croft or here. That's where he keeps his stash." He slapped Jamie's back. "One day young Ewan Cameron will be a rich man."

Jamie laughed. "He seems clever enough already."

"Aye. This way, Jamie. First, we've got to lose the horses. And then settle in for a long snooze somewhere sheltered. Until nighttime."

"Nighttime? But why?"

"We'll be less conspicuous in the dark. Horses can be heard. Boats not necessarily if you're silent enough. We'll walk down another couple of miles to where I've a boat hidden. We'll take it close to the boathouse and then we'll lose that, too."

"Boats?" Jamie's face turned green. "At night?"

Rory grinned. "Ah, there's a first time for everything." He watched the lad's cheeks go from green to scarlet. "This first time not even Mairi can save you."

"Mairi?" The blush deepened.

"Aye, Mairi. She's a good lassie, Jamie. Imagine what she'd say if she heard you've thrown up on a boat on a calm loch?"

Sparing the lad more discomfort, Rory took the horses from him and walked toward the blacksmith's, chuckling all the way.

***

Catriona woke to a grating sound. A sharp pain in her neck and knees reminded her she'd curled up on the settee in the library, reading. Oh dear, she must have fallen asleep! Blinking, she stretched her legs. The sound of voices brought her fully awake. In the dim light of only a couple of candles, she stared at the fireplace, heart in her mouth. Had the Redcoats discovered the exit? Glancing around the room, she found nowhere to hide. She froze in her seat and stared at the man ducking underneath the lintel. He straightened and stared at her.

"Rory!" Catriona jumped up and rushed to him. She stopped a foot in front of him, her fingers intertwined, not daring to touch him. The look of relief in his eyes gave her hope. "You're back." Tears blinded her as a wave of happiness consumed her. He was home. Now, all was going to be fine.

Rory raised a hand, calloused fingers brushing her cheek. "Aye, I'm home, lass."

The sound of footsteps on stone behind him made him drop his hand and turn. "All safe, Jamie. It's only Catriona." He ushered the boy into the room and, reaching into the fireplace, closed the stone door. The lad nodded, cheeks burning.

Catriona took a step back. She felt bereft when Rory dropped his hand, the fragile bond broken again. "I'm so glad to see you both alive and well." Casting a glance at the close-drawn curtains, she said, "Did you get our message?"

Rory nodded. "Aye. Young Ewan waited for us at Inverlochy."

A sudden fear gripped Catriona. "But you came through the cave. The Redcoats know of it."

He smiled, and her head spun. God, she'd worried so much about him, relying on him to simply return and make everything all right.

"We came through the sparkly cave, Cat. I guess they didn't fancy keeping watch inside a dank, narrow tunnel but I'm sure they're watching the main cave. We must keep away from it." He turned to Jamie. "You go and rest, lad. I'm sure you'll find the bunk bed all ready." He looked at Catriona, eyebrow raised in question.

"Yes," she said, turning to Jamie. "You'll find some water in a bowl in the kitchen to freshen up. We kept it ready for you every night. Here, take this candle."

Jamie gave her a curt bow, and took the lit candle. "Thank you, Miss. Until the morning." Silence fell after he'd closed the door behind him.

Aware of the butterflies doing somersaults in her stomach, Catriona covered it with her hand as she glanced at Rory's face. He had not moved, and his scrutinizing gaze made her shiver. Slowly, he broke the spell and flopped onto the settee by the curtained window, patting the seat next to him. "Come, sit, lassie. I heard you dealt with the soldiers well. Tell me."

Catriona sat on the edge of the seat, careful their legs and hips didn't touch. Despite the gap, the heat Rory exuded overwhelmed her. She took a couple of deep breaths, her gaze never leaving the fireplace. Fiddling with her skirts, she startled when he slid his hand up her back, coming to rest at her neck. His strong fingers gently massaged the pain she'd felt on waking.

Her brain cried out for her to ignore his touch, but her body gave in. She turned to him, wrapped her arms around his neck, and lay her head on his chest. God, she'd missed him so much. Had he missed her, too?

Catriona opened her mouth to speak when Rory closed the gap between them in an instant. His mouth crushed hers, devouring her lips, her tongue. His arms trailed down her back, pulling her closer. He'd missed her, surely. Her heart leapt. Sliding her hands underneath his coat, she slid them around his broad torso, feeling his strong muscles underneath the thin fabric of his shirt. Grime brushed her skin but she did not care. Rory was home. He moaned, his kiss turning soft, playful as his teeth nibbled her lower lip before sending a blazing trail down her neck.

"Cat," he growled, "I've..." He broke off, pushing her away, and stared, their faces but inches apart. His eyes shone with disbelief.

Catriona bit her lip, feeling his gaze turning to her mouth. "What?"

He sat back, releasing her. "I apologize, Catriona. I don't know what's come over me."

She withdrew into the corner of the settee. He'd come back to her only to reject her again. He didn't care after all. Tears strained to break through, and she averted her gaze. There was no hope for them, no hope for a shared future. He didn't want her.

"I saw the Redcoats in the cave." She hesitated, taking a deep breath. "I was worried about you that's why I went back in." Her hand shook as she pointed at the fireplace.

"You were curious, you mean." The sarcastic tone of his voice made her shudder. Why did he despise her so much?

"No, Rory. I wasn't curious. Not this time. I was concerned."

"Alright, then. So, what happened?"

"They were searching for something. I couldn't hear them properly, and when I wanted to go back, I sneezed." Shame suffused her. It was her fault that they'd found the tunnel, found the link to other places. Perhaps even suspected a path to this house. "I'm so sorry," she blurted out, pleading with him. "It's all my fault."

"Nonsense, lass." She heard him sigh. "They'd have found it sooner or later. And you didn't lead them here but took the other turn instead. That was very brave of you given you didn't know where it led."

She laughed, the cynical sound ringing harsh in her ears. "No, I wasn't brave. I was scared. But more so about Auntie Meg if they'd found the link to the house." And for you, she thought, not daring to voice it out loud. She swallowed hard.

He took her hand, holding it between his. "You did the right thing, Catriona, and I'll be forever grateful for that."

Grateful? She nearly screamed. Rory was grateful? Shaking off his hands, she stood and turned to face him. "No need to be grateful, Rory. Auntie Meg's part of my family, after all." *And you're not.*

The notion saddened her. It was time for her to retire. "To cut a long story short, a Major Robertson visited us shortly after my excursion. And he accused you of murder." Catriona shivered as she spoke the hated word. "Up north, near Inverness. A government agent." She wanted Rory to deny it but he remained silent. Desperation rose inside her. Was he guilty after all?

"Tell me," she whispered.

Rory pushed himself off the settee. Weariness surrounded him. She'd just wanted to hold him but that was out of the question. He'd push her away again.

An eyebrow raised, his hands gripped her by the shoulders. "Do you think I did it?"

"Of course not." Catriona dug her fingers into his arms, trying to wrestle him off her and pull him closer at the same time. "I never believed you capable of such a deed. I defended you to Major Robertson."

He glared at her, unmoving. "Did you indeed?" A wolfish grin made her want to scream, to hold him, to shake him into believing her.

"How dare you!" She pushed him away, her body shaking with anger. She stepped backwards until her hands found the solid door behind her. "I don't know why you think so poorly of me, after all I've done for you."

She caught her breath and held up a hand when he took a step toward her, opening his mouth. "Stop! I don't want to hear any more. Clearly you don't care about me. That much I realized tonight. You perceive me to be something I'm not. I did the right thing by you today but enough is enough. Next time the soldiers come asking for you, Rory Cameron, you're on your own."

The look of regret on his face, and his slumped shoulders nearly tore her apart. Her heart wanted to comfort him, but he'd brought it on himself.

He reached out his hand. It was too late.

"I can't take any more." With tears streaming down her cheeks, she grabbed the handle and rushed from the room, slamming the door behind her.

Chapter Fourteen

Rory cursed himself as he slowly ascended the stairs. He was comfortable walking in this house in the dark, an instinct borne from many years of experience. He arrived in his bedroom and closed the door behind him. Leaning against it, he let out a long breath. What the hell had gotten into him? He knew she believed him. After all, she defended him to the major. She'd done it to keep him safe. So why was he being such a bastard?

Snorting, he pushed himself away from the door, and dropped his coat onto a chair he knew stood by the wardrobe. He was an idiot, first almost ravishing her, only to end up accusing her of suspecting him of murder. It clearly outraged and disappointed her. She genuinely believed him innocent? Even after the shots she'd heard in the cave. Even knowing he'd been there but not knowing who fired them.

Perhaps, now she'd leave. He may have finally sent her packing. He ignored the devastation that thought brought on and forced a casual shrug. Good, then he could deal with this sordid mess with a clear head, and prove his innocence.

Rory fell onto the bed and pushed his boots off. He slid out of his shirt and trews and dropped them to the floor. They were filthy, crusted with salt from the sea, and stinking of damp grass. Mairi would not be best pleased with the state of them. Lying back naked, he stretched his limbs. For the first time in many days, his sore muscles relaxed. Seduced by the soft pillows and the scent of lavender strong in his nose, he drifted off to sleep.

The frantic knocking on the door woke him. He opened his eyes to find sunlight streaming into the room through a gap in the curtains. It was later than he wanted to get up. Rory swore, rubbed his eyes, and pushed himself into a sitting position, careful to cover himself.

"Aye, I'm awake. Why the uproar?" he shouted just as the door was thrown open. Mairi stuck her face in, saw him half-tucked underneath the blankets, and rushed in, closing the door behind her.

"Good morning, Rory. I've grave news."

"What happened? Is Auntie Meg unwell?" Relief flooded through him when the girl shook her head and went to pull the curtains open. He flinched at the brightness flooding the room.

"She's fine, though still abed. It's Catriona. She's to go back to Edinburgh."

Rory froze. He should be glad. Was it not for the best, her safety secure? Yet a sense of dread settled in his heart. "Is she, now? I'm surprised it took so long for her to have enough of the country."

But Mairi shook her head, gesturing down the stairs. "No. A man arrived early this morning, Rory. Robbie brought him here, though he is wary of him. I don't like him one bit either. Robbie says her father summoned her back. Something about a wedding to plan." The look she sent him was pleading. What did she want him to do? It was well within Catriona's father's right to see her married off.

But the thought twisted his gut. The vision of Catriona lying in someone else's arms, a lecherous mouth on her full, rounded breasts, filthy hands roaming that delectable body, made him ill.

She was *his*.

His? Rory shook his head, banishing the notion from his mind. She'd never be safe with him.

Mairi was still staring at him. "You have to do something. She belongs here now. And the man that came for her..." She shuddered.

"Mairi, you're rambling. Catriona's home is in the city. But I'll have a word with the man in any event."

Mairi strode to his clothes chest, threw the lid open, and

pulled out a fresh shirt and a pair of trews. She tossed them onto the bed.

"Then you best hurry."

She was out the door the moment he pulled the shirt over his head. As if he did not know time was of the essence. Securing the trews, he stood in front of the faded glass on a shelf by the window. He slid his hands through his thick hair, attempting to tame the ruffled mess. Grinning cynically to himself, he eyed his reflection. Funny how he could not see the guilt and sadness he felt should be plain on his face. He pulled on and fastened his brogues, and left the room without a further glance at the mirror. It was a good thing she was leaving. She'd be safer in Edinburgh. Yet why did it feel so wrong?

As he neared the drawing room, his glance only briefly scanning a grimy travel cloak on a hook at the bottom of the stairs, he heard voices. One was Catriona's. A man cut her short. Rory hovered behind the door standing ajar, listening.

"For the last time, Catriona, you'll accompany me to Edinburgh. The wedding has been arranged for the end of the month so we can't afford to waste any time chatting—as much as I'd like to indulge you."

Rory took an instant dislike to the sound of that voice and the commandeering, arrogant note it held. Anger stirred inside him. Nobody spoke to Catriona like that.

But you did, just last night. He shrugged off the memory, and listened.

"No, I'll never wed you. I hate you." Catriona's voice shook.

With fear?

Rory wasted no more time. Without knocking, he pushed the door open. "Good morning." He leaned against the doorframe. "What's happening here?"

His gaze darted from Catriona's face, ravaged by tears, to the man standing by the armchair. Instant hate suffused him as he took in the stranger's appearance. The once-shiny boots and tan breeches were stained with mud. A long coat, adorned with gold thread and matching buttons, came down to his thighs, yet the most incongruous item was a dark blue, heavily-embroidered velvet waistcoat. A neck cloth of the same color made the thin face look pale—an impression not helped by the lanky hair tied back. A dandy! A city gentleman in all but title. He snorted. The kind he knew well, and took the trouble to steer clear of.

The stranger turned on him. "And you are?"

Rory bowed. His self-assurance gave him an edge. "Rory Cameron, at your service."

The man bristled. "I'm John Henderson, Miss MacKenzie's betrothed."

"Former betrothed." Catriona's body shook. "And I'll never go back, not with you."

Her vulnerability touched Rory. He wanted to rush over to her, to comfort her, but he stayed where he was.

Henderson completely ignored her outburst. The man stood, meeting his gaze, eyes cold as slate. "You must be the step-nephew Angus told me about. Tell me, have you tasted dear Catriona's forbidden fruits yet?"

Rage had him clenching his fists, and Catriona took a tentative step toward him but stopped a few feet away.

But Henderson did not let off. Studying his fingernails, he muttered, "Because I found them quite to my liking."

"John!" Catriona's cheeks turned scarlet. "You didn't get anywhere near me." She looked ready to slap him and Rory placed his hand on her shoulder, holding her back.

"He's not worth it, Catriona."

Henderson's chuckle made his skin crawl. "Oh dear, oh dear. I guess you did have a taste, then. But that's all you're getting." He looked at Catriona. "Naughty girl. You're a strumpet after all."

"You bastard!"

Catriona wrenched free from Rory's grasp and rushed forward. Her fists beat Henderson's chest but in one swift move the man pinned her against his body, his icy glare on Rory.

Anger rose from deep inside Rory, straining to burst out. "I believe you are abusing our Highland hospitality,

Henderson. Let Catriona go and be on your way. I only say this once."

"Mmmhh." Henderson's hand squeezed Catriona's bottom as she wriggled to get out of his grasp. "Aye, girl. You move just like that."

Rory's temper flared. In two strides, he crossed the room ready to kill the man. The loud click only reached his brain the moment he found himself staring down the mouth of a cocked pistol.

"Rory!" Catriona exclaimed as Henderson pushed her away with his free hand, sending her stumbling to the ground.

Rory froze, forcing his mind to calm the fury raging through his veins. He glanced across the room, searching for anything to use as a weapon but nothing was close enough. The man was poised to shoot without warning.

"Steady, Cameron. You don't want the girl crying over your dead body. Catriona, get up."

"No."

Rory suppressed a smile at her defiant voice. She was a brave lass. How did he ever doubt her? He watched, blood pumping in his veins. Steady.

Henderson took a step closer to him. "You don't want your friend here to come to any harm, Catriona. Get up and take this string." With his free hand he pulled a leather thong from his pocket and threw it at her. "Tie him up."

"I—"

"Do it!" Henderson bellowed, the hand holding the pistol shaking.

She stared at Rory wide-eyed, fear mingled with sorrow. "I'm sorry," she whispered.

Now. Rory waited until she came close and then turned and pushed her through the open door. "Go!"

From the corner of his eye, he saw Henderson almost upon him. Then something hit his skull, and the room went black.

Chapter Fifteen

"Rory." Mairi's whisper held a note of urgency as strong fingers shook his shoulder. "Rory, come to."

"Mairi? What is it?" He gasped as her fingers dug deep into his upper arm. His head pounded, his eyes unwilling to open. He blinked, and stared at her.

Why was he lying on the floor? He glanced around the room. The drawing room. He swore as memories came rushing back.

Catriona.

"Soldiers. Dozens of them." She dashed to the window, keeping to the side of it as she twitched the curtain a fraction of an inch. "Oh, sweet Lord."

Rory shot up, instant pain soaring through his head. Gently, he touched the side. As he checked his fingers, blood clung to it. Henderson. The bastard!

"Mairi, where's Catriona?"

She shook her head, frowning. "That man Henderson took her. He pointed a pistol at us and dragged her away with him. The next thing I knew the Redcoats are headed our way. You must hurry."

The urgency in her voice cleared his head.

Redcoats!

"Here, I've brought your weapons." Mairi held his sword and cocked pistol ready for him. "The tunnel."

He raced along the hall. Mairi was right behind him, intent to shut the door to the tunnel once he'd gone through. But a sound from the kitchen made him stop. A muffled scream.

Jamie.

The soldiers must have gained entry already and overpowered him. Rory swore. He had to save the lad.

"Cameron?" An impervious voice called from the kitchen. The door opened to reveal the morning light within. Rory wondered how many soldiers hid out of his sight. The sight of Jamie stumbling forward, a dirk at his throat held by a Redcoat behind him, quashed any hopes of escape. "Drop your weapons, or I'll send your boy here to hell." Jamie's eyes widened as a nick in his skin began to bleed.

"Robertson, you bastard!" Mairi shouted and darted forward. Rory grabbed her arm and pulled her back. "Stay! They're here for me. You need to look after Auntie Meg."

"But—"

"Quiet, woman! For once, know an order when it's given," he barked. This was the inevitable moment he'd been dreading for many years.

"Don't do it, Rory. It's not worth it." Jamie's desperate attempt at sacrifice tore at Rory's heart. The boy was prepared to die for him. He'd not allow it.

"Let the boy go." He dropped his sword and pistol to the floor. A sharp look at Mairi stopped her from grabbing the gun.

Raising his voice, he warned the soldiers, "I'm coming into the kitchen now. Let the boy go."

"Who are you to give orders, Cameron? Step over the threshold, arms raised behind your head."

Rory did as he was told and stopped inches in front of Jamie. "Now let him go," he addressed the senior officer, a major, standing next to the lad.

The major nodded to the soldier who withdrew the hand holding the dirk, only to let the handle come crashing down on Jamie's skull. He slumped to the floor at Rory's feet.

Rory glared at the major. "Was that really necessary?" He didn't react when two soldiers took his arms and tied them behind his back. To his relief, Jamie was still breathing, but blood poured from a small gash. Mairi would look after him. He turned his head toward the door where the girl stood, shaking. Behind her, he saw Auntie Meg approaching. She was clutching a woollen wrap as she came to a halt in the doorframe.

"Major Robertson, what is the reason for this intrusion?" Auntie Meg stared at the commotion, her chin thrust forward in a stubborn manner, her whole demeanor haughty.

"Apologies, ma'am." Major Robertson gave a curt bow. "I have an arrest warrant here for Mr Rory Cameron. He's to be taken to Edinburgh under suspicion of smuggling and..." He paused for effect. "The more serious charge of murder."

"Murder?" The old lady shook her head. "I still don't believe it."

"I'm afraid I'm very serious indeed, my lady. We must leave at once." He ushered his soldiers out of the kitchen, his gaze meeting Rory's. "The hangman awaits your company."

***

A week later they approached the boundaries of Edinburgh. Seeing the always increasing, yet familiar outline of buildings, Catriona swallowed hard and kept a firm hold of the reins to stop from screaming. Throughout the long days in the saddle, she refused to speak a word with John. By maintaining a stoic silence all the way, she riled him to no small measure. But she did not get any satisfaction from it as he'd claimed in response that her stupid behavior only made things worse. A gleam in his eyes warned her of exactly what he meant by that. The threat hung over her like a death sentence.

Catriona gazed at the tall buildings, rows upon rows rising toward the castle high on the steep hill ahead. The sight always made her shudder. She knew the narrow closes where tradesmen plied their wares were full of filth- human and animal. How horrible it must be to spend your life in those dark, cold flats! Fortunately, her family home was to the far side of Castle Hill, away from the reeking lanes. She averted her gaze toward the lush countryside surrounding the city, meadows and fields, stretching toward the far hills to the south.

When they arrived at her home, Catriona pulled her skirts together and heaved herself off her horse, giving John no chance to come near her, or, God forbid, touch her. Ignoring the searing pain in her legs, she rushed up the stairs and knocked on the door. A girl Catriona did not recognize opened the door and curtsied. A new maid?

"Good day, Miss Catriona." She smiled. "Welcome home."

Catriona stared at her. She was not in the mood for smiling. "Who are you?"

"I'm Jenny, Miss. I'm new here. Mr Angus gave me this job only last week." The girl blushed and lowered her gaze to the floor.

Ah, another one of Angus' harlots. Catriona sighed, brushed past her, and, removing her gloves, entered the wide hall. She handed them to the maid and attacked the pins that held her hat in place. As she heard John's footsteps echo in the hallway behind her, she dropped the pins onto the floor and threw her hat to the maid.

"Thanks, Jenny. I'll be in my room." After taking the first few steps, she turned, frowning at John. "Indisposed." With that, she ran up the stairs. Let John complain to Angus, or to Father. She needed to think. Reaching her bedroom door, Catriona darted inside and turned the key. For the moment, she was safe. Only slowly did she dare to release her held breath.

At eight of the clock that evening Catriona entered the dining parlor, dressed in a gown the shade of midnight blue, its short, puffed lace sleeves barely covering her arms. Pale yellow underskirts provided a playful contrast to the stark color of the skirts. She'd made an effort with her appearance, not wishing to disappoint her parents who strangely enough had not come to greet her. Not even her mother. A sense of loneliness washed over her.

Catriona stared at the large mahogany dining table. It was set for three. Only three? Was her brother out of town? Perhaps he dined at his club. She strolled over to the matching sideboard and helped herself to a glass of sherry. Sipping, she turned when the door opened. Angus and John entered the room, and she nearly choked. Where were her parents?

"Hello, dear sister," Angus drawled. Clearly, he'd already partaken in some spirits. So much for his *good intentions.*

John seemed equally cheerful. "Hullo, m'dear." He came to a halt next to her, pouring generous measures of brandy into two glasses before handing one to Angus.

Catriona stiffened when his arm brushed hers. She took a step back, not wanting him close. "What's this?" she asked Angus as her hand made a wide sweep that included him and John. "Where are Mother and Father?" Her suspicions rose with Angus' smirk. What was her dastardly brother up to now?

"Ahhh, you see, sister." Angus slumped into the chair at the head of the table, his gaze never leaving hers. "Our dear parents should by now have arrived in London."

"London?" Catriona swayed, her hand seeking the solid wood of the sideboard to steady herself. "Why are they in London? Has something happened?" She caught a glance between the two men. The chuckling sound coming from John made her shudder. Heart in her mouth, she put her glass down and confronted her brother, hands on hips.

"Our parents *did* know I was returning? Did they not?"

Angus' grin told her. "No." He laughed out loud. "They'd only have been in the way. It didn't take much effort to convince them to take a break in London. Father was craving news of a different kind to that of his daughter playing the strumpet."

The slap rang loud in the room. Her hand hurt, but with no small measure of satisfaction she noticed his cheek turning a flaming crimson. "You—"

"Hold your horses, sister." He nodded to John who came up behind her, holding her firmly by the arms as he positioned his body close behind hers. Bile rose in her throat.

Angus rose to stand barely an inch in front of her. Fumes of alcohol assailed her as he spoke. "I warned you, up north. You didn't listen. See, John and I made a little pact. Forget Francis and the others. I gave him contacts, names of some well-known Highlanders, so he can get something he desperately wants—apart from you—and in return he'll marry you despite your ruined reputation. After all, he tasted the goods, so he might just as well enjoy the full meal." Angus grinned and raised his hand. Catriona flinched. He laughed out loud as his smooth palm stroked her cheek.

Fury made her shake, her heart pounding in her ears. How dare he! John's fingers were digging deep into her flesh. He relished the chance to take her, married or not. And with Father away, nobody was left to come to her aid. "And what do you get out of it, Angus? Money?"

He returned to his seat, a look of deep content on his face. "Life is expensive, sister." Raising his glass, he toasted her.

John turned her to face him. He snaked his arms around her, and pulled her into a tight grip, grinding his hip into her stomach. As she felt his arousal, desperation overwhelmed her, making her anger soar. With her fists against his chest, she tried to push him away but he proved surprisingly strong.

"What do you want, John?" Her voice was no more than a hoarse whisper.

"A small token of your affection, dearest bride." His mouth came crashing onto hers. She pressed her lips shut, deep revulsion spreading through her.

Shifting her face to the side, she whispered, "Never."

His hand came up and held her head fast by the chin. "Ooohh, a Highland wildcat. I like that." His lips covered hers again. Catriona gritted her teeth. The sheer force of it stunned her. Why did Angus not do anything? Was he so much in the man's debt? John's tongue delved into her mouth, seeking hers. She saw her chance. With all the anger built up inside her she bit down. When John pushed her away, Catriona let go.

His hand covered his mouth. Blood leaked through his lips.

"Bitch!"

He lunged at her but she scurried around the dining table. Hampered by drink, he stumbled across the floor. Throwing the door open wide, she nearly slammed it in his face before she fled up the stairs. Clutching her skirts, she ran to her bedroom. She ran for her life. His ragged voice followed her, screaming and swearing. With shaking hands, she turned the key in the lock. Surely, even with her parents away he wouldn't dare break the door.

But silence descended. Her ear on the door, she caught her breath. Calm. She must calm herself. The quiet unnerved her. What was he up to now? With much effort, she pushed a small chest of drawers in front of the door. That should keep him out. With a ragged cry, she fell on the bed. What was she to do?

***

Weary from the rough journey, Rory dropped onto the bench in the dank cell they'd thrown him. The last remnants of daylight filtered through the narrow bars from the small window high up, barely reaching into the confined space. Rivulets of slimy water trickled down the rough walls in places. The stink from a bucket in a corner made him gag. His clothes were as filthy as this hovel from days spent riding in rain and gales.

He was used to the fickle weather, but the harsh treatment meted out by Major Robertson surprised him. How the man must despise Highlanders. Each night he left Rory to sleep out of doors, chained to a wall, a tree, a fence without cover from the elements, his shirt ripped and trews sodden with mud. Once a day he was fed gruel. It always gave him stomach cramps but he ate to keep his strength up. When he asked for water after a long, strenuous ride, he'd ended up punished for insolence. His back still burned from the sting of the whip, the inflamed scars a constant reminder.

Carefully, Rory leaned against the wall, only to bolt forward as the sores scraped against the rough surface. He pushed the smelly blanket off the bunk and lay on his arm, keeping himself on his side. Taking a deep breath through cracked lips, he closed his eyes. He needed a miracle.

A vision of Catriona came unbidden. He moaned as he remembered the man who abducted her. Henderson must have taken her to Edinburgh. So near yet so far. His own helplessness shamed him, and the thought of Henderson forcing himself on Catriona sickened him. He was unable to save himself, never mind the lass. He balled his hands into fists as he imagined her fighting spirit subdued, molded to respond to the man's every whim. He shook his head, clearing his mind of the thought.

'Twas all his fault.

A slim shaft of sunlight fell onto the floor when he awoke the next morning to the sound of a key grating in the lock. Groaning, he pushed himself into a sitting position as the door opened. A gaoler, clad in filthy rags, shuffled into the cell with a plate of stale bread and a pitcher of water, followed by a soldier with a cocked pistol aimed at Rory.

"Thank you," Rory whispered, his throat dry from the lack of water. He grabbed the pitcher and drank greedily. The gaoler pulled it from him and set it on the floor. "Too much water and ye'll kill yersel'." His gaze surveyed Rory's appearance. "Had a rough trip?"

Rory gave a croaky laugh. "Aye, you could say so."

The man nodded. "Major Robertson doesn't take prisoners. If ye ken wha' I mean."

Rory understood. "I'm still alive."

"Just," the gaoler replied and waddled off toward the heavy door, followed by his shadow, the pistol never leaving Rory. "Ye're due in court tomorrow afternoon before Judge Lawson." The door banged shut.

Rory groaned and dropped his head into his hands. He'd heard of the judge. Judge Lawson hated Highlanders. He was the one who sent Rory's associates to the gallows. And he'd happily send him after them. His miracle better hurry before the noose tightened around his neck.

***

Catriona woke to the sounds of birds singing outside her window. Daylight flooded the room. She raised her hands to shade her eyes from the glare. Barely open, they began to stream. Gently, her fingers probed the puffed lids when memory came rushing back. The reason she cried herself to sleep. John and Angus scheming. Mother and Father in London. How could she have fallen into such a trap?

A soft knock on her door made her jump. "Go away." Her voice croaky, she barely managed a whisper.

"Good morning, Miss Catriona," the new maid called cheerfully, her knocks growing insistent. "Let me in. You'll need help with your morning toilette."

"I don't need any help," Catriona cried. "I'm staying abed today. I'm not well."

"The more reason to let me in, Miss. I can look after you."

Catriona didn't miss the urging tone in Jenny's voice. The girl must be desperate, probably under Angus' instructions.

As if to confirm her suspicions, she heard frantic whispers coming from the corridor. She slid out of bed and tiptoed to the door. Sitting on the chest of drawers she'd pushed to bar it, she leaned her ear against the wood. 'Twas as she thought. Her brother's voice rose harsh against the maid's whimpering. A slap from the other side made Catriona jump. Her hands flew to her mouth. All the devils in the world could not make her shift that chest. It was her only protection.

"Open the door, Catriona." The threat in his voice was unmistakable.

"Get lost, Angus!"

"All right, then. I'll come in." The knob turned and a thump hit the door.

"You won't be able to. I've moved furniture in front of the door. You won't shift it." Still, she jumped when his fists rained down on the shaking wood. Praying it would hold, she looked around the room for other items to block the door. But the bed and wardrobe were solid, too bulky, and the light French desk was far too flimsy. Her heart beat in her ears as the pounding on the door ceased, and silence descended. Heavy footsteps retreated along the corridor, followed by a lighter step.

Heaving a sigh of relief, Catriona sat on the bed. She was

a prisoner in her own home, her own bedroom. No food. No water. No comforts. Cursing her brother, she chewed at her fingernails. She needed to find a way out.

Her gaze fell on the balcony doors.

Chapter Sixteen

Rory woke with another pounding headache. His sleep disturbed, not only by noises outside his cell door all night but by his own memories. Catriona's voice invaded his dreams as he approached the gallows, calling his name, urging him to step back. Noose tight around his neck, a vision of her gold-flecked eyes, tears streaming down her cheeks, jolted him back into the dim morning light casting shadows in his prison.

He closed his eyes again. The girl's life was ruined, and all because his jealousy had got the better of him. Henderson wound him up, toying with Catriona right under his nose, until he walked right into the trap. Rory shook his head, relishing the stabs of pain at his temples. Oh, he deserved the pain. Because of his foolish action the girl was in the hands of that lecherous bastard.

Anger raged through him like a wildfire at the thought of Henderson's hands on Catriona's helpless body, her silent screams echoing through his head. He'd take the look of dread, of fear on her beautiful face to his grave. She'd counted on him and, in his jealousy, he made a mistake. He let her down. Now it was too late, not only for him, but also for her. Yet while he'd be dead, her whole life still lay ahead of her. A life of misery and shame. A lifetime of abuse. Rory jumped up and kicked the bunk, wood splintering into shards. His fists pummeled the cell door but not a sound emerged from the other side. His curses went unanswered. Drained of all energy, he collapsed and leaned against the damp wall, its rough edges digging into his scars. He didn't care. Closing his eyes, he let the grief flow through him. She was out of his reach. Forever.

The rattle of a key in the door jolted him awake. He must have dozed off—but for how long? Rory stood, staring at the damage he'd done to himself. His knuckles beaten raw, and his calves were smeared with blood from the sharp chunks of wood. The bunk lay in a sorry pile. He stepped back as the door opened, and his gaoler entered with a jug of water and a loaf.

As expected, the soldier with the pistol came in to prevent any attack. Surely, they'd heard his earlier rant. The gaoler eyed the splintered bunk and put the food and water down without a word. He picked up yesterday's dishes and turned to speak to a man hidden in the shadows of the corridor. "Ye can come in now. At yer own risk." He stepped aside as Major Malcolm Campbell stepped over the threshold, an eyebrow raised as he surveyed the damage.

"You gone raving mad already, Rory?" A smirk touched the corners of his mouth. "Leave us," he ordered the gaoler. The man scuttled out. "You too." The soldier's gaze cast a doubtful glance at Rory.

"Are you certain, Sir? Cameron might attack you."

"Cameron won't harm me. Now go on a round of the building, and don't dare come back before I call for you!" A scowl from the senior officer made the soldier turn on his heel, slamming the door shut behind him, key grating in the lock. Malcolm waited until the footsteps retreated down the corridor, then let out a long breath.

"You're in a big mess, Rory." He clasped Rory's arm.

"Aye, I know. I haven't got much time." Rory dragged his hand through his hair. Embarrassment suffused him. He turned away from his friend, squinting into the light seeping through the bars.

A sharp hiss from Malcolm reminded him of his scarred back. Of course, the linen was torn and bloody from the marks underneath. "I'll make a fine picture of a man before Judge Lawson," he said bitterly, his hands gripping the bars.

Malcolm stepped to his side, a gentle hand on his shoulder. Rory shrugged it off. He didn't deserve his friend's sympathy.

"Get a hold of yourself." Malcolm's voice was calm, yet sharp. Of course, he *was* used to giving orders. Rory snorted.

"To what effect? I'm going to die." His gaze met his friend's before he lowered them. "I've let the cause down. And I've let Catriona down," he added with a whisper.

"Who did this to you? Robertson?" Malcolm swore when Rory nodded. "The bastard has no friends up north. He knows how to make Highlanders appear like wild animals before Judge Lawson. Suits both of them." The contempt in Malcolm's voice made Rory look at him again.

"Robertson's doing this on purpose? Making me look like an animal to give the judge justification?" Rory could hardly believe it but Malcolm nodded.

"Not all military men share his views. You know I don't."

"I know. You're not to blame." He straightened himself and turned. "Why are you here anyway? I'm beyond help."

"I don't think so." Malcolm turned and let his gaze roam the room. "You've had your chance to let off steam. Now we're going to get you out of here."

"What?" Rory's laugh echoed through the room. "Lawson has yet to free a Highlander accused of murder."

"Don't worry about that. It's in hand." Malcolm's eyes lit up, a cunning smile on his lips.

"What are you up to now? Don't get yourself into trouble on my behalf, Malcolm." Rory shook his head. His friend was always one for surprises but this time it had to be more than just a ruse. He needed proof.

Malcolm chuckled. "Well, it'll all turn out fine, you trust me." His expression turned serious. "I have proof of the Edinburgh banker who had his sights on your muskets. His spies have kept an eye on you for many months, following your trail, but he still hasn't found what he most covets. He gave your name to Robertson in the hope the good major would make you spill the beans."

"Robertson never asked about the muskets." Rory stared at his friend. He marveled at Malcolm's efficiency. The major's network of spies must be the envy of kings.

"No, because he's not interested enough. He doesn't

believe they exist so he brought you here to get rid of one very influential Highlander. I bet our banker friend isn't best pleased because for him your death means the end of the road. No muskets." He grinned. "I've lodged the papers with the name of the real murderer to the judge. At first Lawson didn't want to know—as you can imagine—but in the end he was forced to believe me. I've given him the name of the culprit, a crooked Inverness lowlife, and he's now been detained. Didn't take long for him to sing."

"So I'm free to go?" Rory's hopes soared. Perhaps he might still help Catriona. His heart began to race but Malcolm's next words sobered him.

"No. The trial is still going ahead but it's a foregone conclusion. However, you're still wanted for smuggling," Malcolm said, his voice turning to a whisper. He glanced toward the door before leaning closer to Rory. "But I have a plan."

"A plan?"

"Don't interrupt. Listen, and for once just do as you're told. I've added a note to the murderer's file that he was involved in hiding the Spanish muskets."

"You did *what*?" Rory shook his head.

"Shut up and listen." Malcolm paused. "I'm afraid you'll have to give me the muskets."

"Never! You know they're for—"

"I'm fully aware of their purpose." Malcolm sighed. "But in order to save your neck, you have to give them up."

"Malcolm, I can't. We'll need them." Rory stared at his friend. How could he ask this of him? A successful rising was only months away. He knew it.

"There won't be another rebellion, Rory. The chiefs have withdrawn from the cause to continue their own petty wars. Scotland's in English hands now."

Rory could not bear to hear more. He rubbed his hands over his eyes. Tired, his shoulders slumped, heavy with the burden of failure. His whole life's purpose was winning a free Scotland. He had already survived one rebellion. He expected to live through another or at least die trying. Now that was not to be. A dark cloud descended on him, crushing his heart.

"Still, someone's going to need them one day." Desperation choked him. His breath came out in short, ragged bursts. He was not one to quit.

Malcolm shook his head. "It's your life or the muskets. Your decision." He turned toward the door and banged a fist against it. "Open up! And bring me my bag." Footsteps hurried toward the door, and it creaked open. The soldier handed Malcolm a large bundle. "Thanks. Now wander slowly to the end of the corridor, and then come back for me." The soldier nodded and shut the door. Malcolm threw the bag onto the remnants of the bunk.

"A change of clothes. If I'd known you were wounded, I'd have brought bandages. At least now you'll look more presentable before the judge."

Rory shuffled toward the bunk, his mind numb. He pulled a clean, white shirt from the bag. "What a shame this will be bloody within the hour."

"Hurry. I'm going to take your dirty clothes with me."

Rory gingerly removed the ripped shirt. Malcolm swore as the extent of the punishment Major Robertson meted out was thrust in front of his eyes.

"The bastard. If I only knew yet how to stop him."

"Nobody can stop men like Robertson." Rory pulled the fresh shirt over his head, the scent of lavender soap sharp in his nose. Good. At least, he'd not smell like a sewer rat. "They thrive under this government." Hate flooded him at the injustice of it all. He dropped his dirty trews onto the floor and slipped into the tan breeches he'd pulled from the bag. Stockings, a greatcoat, a neckerchief, and a pair of black boots, polished to shiny perfection, completed the change. Grimacing, he scratched at the stubble on his chin and cheeks.

"Sorry, I wasn't allowed to bring a sharp knife for shaving. But tame your hair." He fished a leather strap from his pocket and handed it to Rory. Taking the strap between his teeth, Rory raked his hands through his hair until the last rebellious strands were smoothed back. Swiftly, he tied it in a knot.

"All for nothing, anyway, my friend." He watched Malcolm push his dirty clothes and brogues into the bag, lacing it up.

"Why?" Malcolm's eyes glinted with suspicion.

"I can't reveal the hiding place. It's for the best." He sighed. "Go and see Jamie MacKinnon when the time is right. Be that next year or the next decade."

"You stubborn fool," Malcolm growled at him. In two strides he was confronting Rory, digging his hands deep into his shoulders. Rory closed his eyes as pain tore through him.

"It's for the best," he repeated. Malcolm's fist came out of nowhere, hitting his gut hard. He doubled over while Malcolm stepped back.

"So you're sacrificing yourself, is that it?" Malcolm laughed out loud, the sound devoid of any mirth. "What pretence! Those muskets won't be worth much in ten, twenty years' time. They'll be rusty and the powder damp."

"No." Slowly straightening up, Rory shook his head. "It won't be that long."

"Listen to me." Malcolm stood nose to nose with him now. "I refuse to let you throw away your life for naught. What about Lady Meg? And Jamie? They rely on you."

Rory leveled his gaze to his friend's irate stare. "They'll be fine. I've made sure of that."

"Have you, now?" Malcolm's expression turned cynical. "And what about the young lass you mentioned earlier? Miss Catriona?"

Rory's breathing stopped. What indeed? She'd be left to rot at the hands of that bastard. But what was he to do? *Nothing.* Stubbornly, he shook his head again. "By now, she's probably wed to that bastard, Henderson."

"Henderson?" Malcolm's eyebrows shot up.

"Aye, some dandy banker friend of her brother's. He took her from *Taigh na Rhon*."

"A banker? By name of Henderson? His given name isn't John, by chance?" Malcolm's body tensed.

"Aye, that's him." Seeing recognition in Malcolm's eyes,

Rory groaned as the truth hit him. "He's not the one after my muskets, is he?"

A wolfish grin on his friend's face told him he was right. "Aye, the man who got you arrested, and accused of murder. The man who wants your muskets. John Henderson."

Rory squared his shoulders as realization hit him. "What have I done? I've left her to that devil." Rage returned with a vengeance.

Malcolm gently patted his shoulder, careful not to touch his wounds. "And now you'll save her from his clutches. They're not wed yet. In fact, we're trying to find him. Any ideas?"

"Probably near the MacKenzie town house." The terror he'd seen in her eyes now made sense. Henderson was not just a lecherous dandy. He was a plotter and a killer. "What does he want the guns for?"

Malcolm spat into the corner and wiped his mouth with the back of his hand. "To sell to the highest bidder, of course. He's a dealer."

Urgency unlike he had ever felt gripped Rory. He was helpless, stuck in this cell. And Catriona was in the clutches of an evil man. Malcolm was right. They must find Henderson—before the bastard had a chance to do any more damage to Catriona. The sudden glimmer of hope gave him back his energy. He was ready to go. When he found her, he'd take her back home.

"Now I've got you back," Malcolm exclaimed. He tilted his head toward the door. "The guard'll be back any second. Where are the muskets?"

The blasted arms versus Catriona's life. In a heated whisper, Rory revealed all, and nothing he'd done in his entire life felt so right. The need to save her from Henderson's clutches overwhelmed him, throwing him into a maelstrom of plans. His mind buzzing, he shook Malcolm's hand as they parted ways.

"See you in court, my friend."

"Aye," Rory replied. "We shall meet there." But his thoughts had already left the filthy cell behind.

***

Darkness descended over the rooftops of the houses around them, yet a sliver of daylight remained. The mild summer breeze ruffled the leaves of the birch tree in front of her balcony. Catriona changed into a plain linen dress and riding boots, leaving her stays behind, their stiffness a hindrance. She'd only packed a small bundle of essential garments, her cloak, and mittens. Excitement mingled with apprehension. What if something went wrong? She might die on the stone terrace below her. Or be attacked on her way to the Highlands. Determined to make it all work out, she shrugged off any doubts. She leaned over the railing of the balcony but below all windows lay in darkness. Angus must have gone out.

From inside her bedroom, she took the blankets she'd knotted together earlier today. Ignoring her rumbling stomach, she tested the strength of the knots a final time before tying one end around an iron bar in the corner of the balcony's railing. Bracing her feet against the wrought iron, she leaned back with all her weight. The knot held. With a final glance at the deserted terrace and garden, she let the blankets drop. They fell just short of the floor, but close enough for her to get to the ground safely.

Catriona drew the curtains before closing the balcony doors behind her. She threw her bundle over the railing. It landed with a thud. Listening for sounds from below, she held her breath and only let it out slowly when nothing moved. *Now or never.*

Skirts lifted, Catriona raised one leg over the railing. She clung to the metal while she heaved her other leg over. A quick glance told her the distance to the ground. *Best not look down.* She crouched low, careful not to step onto the hem of her dress, and took hold of the blanket. Fear seized her heart as her other hand let go of the safe metal, to cling on to the bedcover.

Dear God, please!

With a prayer heavenward, she closed her eyes and eased herself off the balcony floor. Dangling in the air, her hands dug deep into the sheets as they swayed violently. Sweat beaded her brow and hands, threatening to make her fingers too slippery to hold on. Finally, her feet found a knot, and she dragged herself downwards, inch by inch, knot by knot.

After what seemed an eternity, a ripping sound made her look up. It was too dark to see where the cloth ripped but she knew she needed to hurry. Looking down, relief flooded through her. The ground was mere feet away. With a final effort, she let go of the sheets and tumbled to the stone terrace. Scared in case someone heard her, she froze. Silence still surrounded her. Scrambling to her feet, she grabbed the bundle and slung it over her shoulder.

Catriona hurried along the gardens, glad of the many times she'd wandered through them in the dark. The faint light barely outlined the trees. The croaking of the frogs told her how close she was to the pond. On another occasion, she'd have loved to sit and listen to the natural world around her. But not tonight. She swallowed hard. She'd never enjoy this peaceful retreat again.

The hedges grew thicker when she neared the far wall, with its locked door leading to the fields beyond. She'd have to skirt the city but her mind was made up. The coin she'd kept hidden in her wardrobe for so long was now sewn into her cloak, just enough to get her to Loch Linnhe. Once at the manor, Auntie Meg was bound to help her.

Memory of *Taigh na Rhon* brought back the pain Catriona felt when John forced her from her new home. Fear for Rory was eating away at her insides. She briefly closed her eyes and prayed he was still alive. Determined to see him again once she was back in the Highlands, she forced her worry for him from her mind, and approached the gate. Angus often crept in through it, so it would be unlocked. Slowly, she pulled it open. On tiptoes, she sneaked through and carefully shut it behind her. Breathing a sigh of relief, she turned. A shadow of a large man loomed over her.

"What—?"

He threw a coarse sack over her head. She lashed out at solid muscle but a rope tied swiftly around her pushed her arms against her body. John must have arranged for someone to keep watch. Well, she'd show them! She kicked out, cursing her skirts as her toes connected to a shin.

"Little witch. You won't do that again." Something hard hit her head.

Chapter Seventeen

Rory stood with his head held high when Judge Lawson, his fleshy head topped by a powdered wig, entered the courtroom, his bulky frame looming large as he waddled to his seat.

So, this was the man who'd sent so many brave Highlanders to the gallows. Rory watched the judge wriggle himself into a throne-like chair covered in cushions. He was hard-pressed not to laugh at the ridiculous picture in front of him. The man was a caricature, everything he despised in the wealthy and powerful of Edinburgh.

Rory's glance roamed upwards to the empty public benches. A trial behind closed doors. So the judge was not able to make an example of him, otherwise the local press and a number of handpicked citizens would have been invited to watch the spectacle.

The prosecutor eyed him like a hawk ready to pounce on a hapless rabbit. Clearly, here was another monster, baying for Highland blood. Rory's heart plummeted.

Malcolm sat on a bench behind him. Rory scrutinized the lawyer his friend hired. Mr Steele, a stooped, reedy man with a devilishly witty glow in his eyes, had brandished a pair of spectacles at him when they first met only an hour earlier, ranting about the evilness of smugglers and Border Reivers. But by the end of their conversation, Steele jested with him and slapped him on the back in an attempt to cheer him. Only Rory's self-control stopped him from punching the older man in return, his scars livid where the lawyer's hand had hit them. It was not Steele's fault. Rory had not revealed the full extent of his mistreatment. A grimace-like grin was all he could muster.

Now he watched as the wily old fox sparred with the prosecutor, Steele's wrinkly face full of indignation at the false accusation and brutal detention of his client so esteemed by the Lochaber community. Rory suppressed a smirk as Judge Lawson's expression grew more and more exasperated. Everyone in the room knew—or at least guessed—the truth.

Called to give his statement, Malcolm provided a faultless account of his investigations into the murder, and the culprit caught. Dressed in full military regalia, right down to the ceremonial sword by his hip, Malcolm was the model of a government soldier and quite convincing. The judge nodded in agreement at the smooth handling of Malcolm's words in Rory's defense, reluctance written on his features. For the second time, his friend came to his rescue. How could he possibly ever repay him when Malcolm risked his reputation —and possibly even his life—on his behalf?

On hearing a petition from the prosecutor to question Rory, Judge Lawson's gaze fell on him. The jowls wobbled as he nodded at his clerk who duly cleared his throat.

"Step into the witness box, Mr Cameron." Rory glanced briefly at Malcolm before he took the stand. He placed his hand on the Bible the clerk held out, and swore to tell the truth and nothing but the truth. A faint nod from his lawyer should calm him, yet unnerved him. What on earth was going on?

"You are here to answer to charges of murder, Roderick Cameron," Judge Lawson rasped. "How do you plead?"

Rory felt the judge towering over him like a mound of soft flesh. He looked up, meeting the judge's cold eyes. "I am not guilty, your Honor." He held the gaze without blinking, without falter. Inside, his mind was in turmoil. Why was he not accused of smuggling? Did Steele have something to do with it? The judge moved back in his chair and grudgingly gestured for the cross-examination to begin.

The prosecutor stepped forward. "What can you tell me about the deceased, Mr Cameron? You don't deny knowing him?"

"No, I knew him. He was a drover we sometimes

employed to move our cattle to the markets in Stirling and Carlisle." Rory remained calm, the churning in his gut safely suppressed. If he stuck to the basic truth, he might just make it.

"You heard Major Campbell here. He said you reported the death to him, in Inverness. Is that correct?"

"Yes, that is correct. I was on my way to the city on business when I came across the deceased before he was killed. I was conversing with him when a shot rang out from behind me. He died in front of my eyes."

"And you pursued the murderer?" Judge Lawson asked, leaving the prosecutor glaring at him, open-mouthed, clearly incensed at the disruption.

"Aye, your Honor." Rory nodded. The judge's changed demeanor mystified him. Suddenly the balance shifted his way. "By the time I scaled the wall opposite, he'd disappeared. So I thought it best to report the death to the major as promptly as possible."

The prosecutor fiddled with his pencil. "Your Honor—"

"Silence, Cummings! I'm conducting this interview myself from now on, as you can see."

"Yes, my Lord." The prosecutor shrank back into his bench, glaring at Rory.

"Mr Cameron, one thing baffles me. How did you come to know Major Campbell? After all, your clans are not exactly" —he hesitated before adding— "on the same political side."

Rory glanced at his friend. "That's easy to answer, your Honor. Major Campbell saved my life many years ago. Some months later, I was grateful for my chance to return the favor." Malcolm inclined his head in silent solidarity.

"A Cameron with Macdonald blood and a Campbell? Most unusual." The judge leaned back, scratching his chins.

"'Tis so, your Honor." Malcolm stood. "Sometimes fate is stronger than blood feuds."

"Well, not in my experience of the Highlanders, Major Campbell." He dismissed Malcolm, and locked eyes with Rory. "I hear from Major Campbell your quick report led not only to the arrest of the murderer, but also to information the man held about the location of certain Spanish muskets, in traitors' hands since the pathetic attempt at an uprising at Glen Shiel last year. They are recovered as we speak."

Rory kept his breathing steady. This was the cue Lawson had been waiting for. Some sign of Rory's complicity, his guilt, his knowledge of the arms. He held the judge's suspicious gaze calmly.

"So the major tells me. I believe he has served you well, Major Campbell has. He's an extraordinary investigator on behalf of the Crown, your Honor," he added as if as an afterthought. Something shifted in the judge's eyes, from speculation to something akin to...respect? Rory held back a snort, hardly daring to breathe. He was about to learn his fate.

Judge Lawson leaned back, the chair creaking under his weight. "Return to your seat, Mr Cameron." He waited until Rory returned to his bench, flanked by two guards before he took a long look at Malcolm, thoughts hidden with years of practice. With a curt nod at the prosecutor, he said, "I'm now ready to pronounce judgment."

Cummings rose and opened his mouth but Judge Lawson's hand shot up, preventing him from butting in. "Thank you, Cummings. I'm finished with this case."

Rory rose at the clerk's order, his gaze never leaving the judge's face. Lawson held his fate in his fleshy hand. Did he believe him?

"I find the accused, Roderick Cameron," Judge Lawson paused, eyes meeting Rory's in final warning, "not guilty. Mr Cameron, you are a free man." With that, Judge Lawson pushed his bulk from the chair and shuffled through the door behind him without another glance back.

Cummings stalked out the door, clearly in a huff. Rory let out a long breath.

Malcolm came over and clasped his shoulder. "Well done, my friend." His lawyer, Steele, winked, pleased with himself and the story he concocted, and scurried from the Court.

"I owe you, Malcolm. Again." Rory's voice shook. His insides were raw with emotion, convinced the judge still doubted the evidence he'd heard. Yet he set him free.

"You've just saved my life for the second time. This is becoming a habit."

Malcolm laughed out loud and drew Rory with him. Outside the court, Rory gulped in the fresh air. He watched the bustling scene. Gentlemen on horseback wound their way through peddlers' stalls. A herd of cows turned into a narrow close nearby. His gaze fell on a girl heaving a basket full of browned apples across the street. Her long dark hair reminded him of...

"Catriona." Now that he was free he must help her. If it was not too late already. "Have you any news?"

"Come with me," Malcolm said. "We've much to discuss and no time to lose."

***

Catriona drifted out of her daze. She wanted to wipe the grit from her eyes but was unable to move her hands. Her eyes flung open. Pale dimness surrounded her, only a sliver of light filtered through gaps in wooden slats covering a tiny window.

Frightened, she stretched, hoping to get up, only to find her hands bound behind her back, and her legs tied at the ankles, the cord cutting to the bone when she tried to free herself.

"What in God's name?" she muttered.

Panic coursed through her. Her skin crawled. A constant rattling sound tore at her nerves. Rain? A roof? Where was she?

Catriona used her elbow and shoulder to push herself upright. Dizziness overcame her in black waves. She closed her eyes and groaned. Her whole body was on fire but the fierce throbbing at her temple was the worst. Looking at the spot where she'd lain, she gasped at a small, dark patch. Blood. She recoiled and looked around. The room was bare, devoid of furniture. Not even a rug covered the beaten floor.

Then the memory came flooding back, freezing her to the core. Oh, God. She'd been taken just as she was on the verge of escape. *But who...?*

John.

It had to be John. His rage from the night before probably festered. Was Angus involved? Or did he still think her safe in her room, sulking? Surely, someone must have noticed the knotted sheets dangling from her balcony. How much time had passed?

A shuffling sound came from the other side of the solid door. Heavy footfalls on wooden steps. Metal scraped against the door as someone tried to insert the key into the lock, and failed miserably. Catriona slumped back onto the ground and forced her breathing to slow. Keeping her lids half-closed, she stared at the door. Best if whoever came in found her still knocked out.

Dear God, I need a plan.

After much prodding, the key slid into the lock and turned, and the door slammed open, hitting the wall. Rain pounded behind a tall shadow entering the room. John. She'd recognize his hateful shape anywhere. Closing her eyes, she prayed he'd fall for her ruse. His shuffling steps drew nearer yet the sound of the rain didn't fade. He must have left the door open. Perhaps someone would see her? Her breath slowed to almost a halt. Focusing on the steady rise and fall of her chest, she heard his steps approach. Something sharp prodded her in the side. His boot.

Breathe in. And out.

"Bloody useless girl." John's voice was close to her ear, whisky fumes mingled with her calm breath. Drunkard! Nearly retching, she kept her eyes firmly closed.

"Wake up, bitch!" His hand grabbed her shoulder and shook her. "Wake up!" Catriona let him shake her, ignoring the pain at her temples. "No use to me in this state, you are. Well, I have ways to teach you," he growled.

Feeling him lean over her, she took her chance. Her eyes flew open. She pulled her legs up and rammed them into his groin. John dropped to the floor next to her, howling, his hands clutching his crotch.

"Help!" Catriona screamed at the top of her voice. Pushing

herself on her side along the floor, the rough wood scraping her elbow, she inched toward the door. "Somebody help me!"

But then John was upon her, still gasping. He grabbed her by the hair and pulled her back. With a thud, she collapsed onto the floor. Pain shot up her arm as she tried to cushion the fall with her elbows. He pulled her head back. Stars swam in front of her eyes, and the temptation to just let go, to slip into oblivion, was nearly too much to resist. But she needed to keep her wits about her.

"What are you doing? Let me go," she cried through clenched teeth.

A cruel smile curled his thin lips. "I'm doing what I should've done months ago, dearest. I'm going to take what's mine."

Bile rose within her as his filthy breath reached her nose. She turned her face away from him but he pulled it back with a greasy thumb, roughly sliding it over her chin and lower lip. When it pushed between her lips, she bit down, tasting his blood for the second time in two days.

"Bitch!" He slapped her hard and dropped her head to the floor. Her ears rang, and black dots appeared in front of her eyes as she toiled for breath. Kicking at the cords at her ankles, she fumed. There must be a way out.

"Let me go at once," she ordered him. "Angus will come looking for me."

"I think not," John snarled. "Nobody knows where you are, not even your wayward brother. Now I've got an appointment to attend to, but don't worry—you won't have to wait long for me. I'll be back soon to finish what we started those many weeks ago." He stood, leering at her, and strolled to the door. "You might be interested to know that Rory Cameron's trial was held this morning. I'm certain his execution's going to attract quite a crowd at the Grassmarket. I, for one, will be cheering when he dangles at the end of that rope."

"Rory...executed?" Catriona whispered. The thought of Rory's body hanging lifelessly from the gallows shook her to the core. The truth hit her harder than John's hand had moments earlier. She'd have lied to the Court to keep him from harm, just like she lied to Major Robertson. Now he was going to die, alone. Tears stung in her eyes, as she glared at John's retreating frame. "You bastard! You'll pay for this."

His snigger chilled her, sending icy shivers down her spine. John fooled them all—society, her parents, maybe even her clueless brother.

"My dear, Catriona, your allegiance is moving. But remember, you're *mine* now—not Cameron's, and when I return from his execution I'll show you what that means." He took the key and grabbed the door handle. The solid wood banged into place. The sound of the key grating in the lock ended her hopes of escape. Clearly, despite his inebriation, he was not too drunk to forget to lock her in.

Catriona let the tears fall freely as she curled up on the barren floor, her body shaking. A sense of loss descended on her. She imagined Rory led to the gallows, the noose tightened around his neck, the ground opening beneath his feet.

"Rory." She sobbed. "You can't die." The only man she trusted. The only man she loved.

Dead.

Chapter Eighteen

"Taken? What do you mean, taken?" Rory stared at Malcolm, heart missing a beat, as they rushed toward the stable where Malcolm left two horses.

"My spy reported watching a scuffle at the garden gate of the MacKenzie property a couple of nights ago. Miss MacKenzie had not been seen out of doors since her return. I believe she was locked up. And then, this commotion. It confirms my suspicion." Malcolm gestured to a stable lad to bring their mounts.

"And?" Rory glowered at his friend. An urgent need flowed through him, feeding his rage.

"Well, someone was caught by the gate. My spy said he heard a muffled cry but as there were three attackers, he couldn't come to her aid. I assume John Henderson was behind it. No-one else has any reason to abduct her."

"Henderson again," Rory growled. Fear gnawed at his insides, and his blood boiled.

Malcolm settled into the saddle. "Come, Rory. The noose is tightening around Henderson's neck."

"Where are we going?" Rory asked as sat up. Gingerly, he straightened, his scars itching. Irritated, he stopped short of scratching his own back and followed Malcolm from the stable.

"I have in my possession a paper that details all of the Henderson family properties. But first we'll pay a visit to young MacKenzie's home." Malcolm strode ahead, up the cobbled streets toward the new-built houses set away from the dank, packed flats on castle hill.

As they turned the horses toward the rows of new manors springing up on the lower side of town, Rory's pulse raced.

The pain from the scars fought with his rage at himself for having left Catriona to her fate. It only fed his fury at Angus.

What kind of brother was he, to allow his little sister to be the puppet in his game? A gambler. A wastrel. A dandy. Revulsion tore through Rory's blood as he urged his mount down the street, dodging merchant carts, cattle, and beggars. Grand buildings, several stories high, with elaborate paintwork and plastering, proved the city's better fortunes following the union. He snarled. All earned on the broken backs of the poor folk.

Rory and Malcolm stood at the bottom of the steps leading to the double doors painted in shiny black, an ornate gilt knocker resting on the varnished wood. He took a deep breath and climbed the steps at a slow pace in an attempt to keep his temper in check. His back straight, the tension almost tore him apart. Swallowing hard, he lifted and dropped the knocker, and took a step back. Within seconds, a young maid opened the door, furtively wiping her eyes with the back of her hand. Raising her head, her lips parted in a shy smile.

"Good afternoon, sirs."

"Good afternoon," Rory answered. "I wish to speak to Angus MacKenzie." Not giving her time to form an excuse, he stepped across the threshold, brushing past her.

"I'm sorry, but Mr Angus is out. And...and he is not expected back till later tonight." She lowered her gaze, her hand still resting on the doorknob.

"No worries. I'll find him." Rory walked toward the first door and flung it open. The lavishly furnished drawing room was empty. He turned and listened at the door across the corridor. A faint grating sound caught his ear, almost imperceptible. "Angus!"

"S-s-sir, 'tis as I said, Mr Angus is out. Will you please leave?"

Rory rounded on her. "I don't care what you say. He's here, and I'll find him." He moved her out of his way and grabbed the handle of the door. It was locked.

"What's in here?"

"The library, sir. Nobody uses it these days." Her voice trembled. She hesitated, clearly under pressure from Angus.

"Unlock the door," Malcolm ordered. The girl's shoulders shook but Rory felt no sympathy. She may have been involved in Cat's abduction.

"I can't, sir. I don't have a key."

"Angus," Rory yelled at the top of his voice. The girl scurried over to stand in front of the library door.

"Sir, please. Nobody's in."

"Where's Miss Catriona?" He closed in on her, inches separating them, until she was forced to tilt her head back to meet his gaze. Quickly, she lowered it again, fiddling with her apron.

"Miss Catriona's out, too. Riding in the park."

"A lie!"

The maid's head shot up. Rory took her by the shoulders and moved her to the side, out of his way, and his gaze settled on the solid wood. "Miss Catriona has been abducted."

"No!" The girl's voice faltered. She seemed to crumple against the wall.

"Yes indeed, so you should be forthcoming with the key immediately." Malcolm's warning made the maid shrink even further.

"I...I really don't have it, sir." She sobbed.

"Angus," Rory roared. Glaring at the maid, who'd cowered behind the banister, he took a step back. With his blood at boiling point, his boot hit the door, and the crack of breaking wood reverberated along the hall. "Come out, you coward!"

He kicked the door again and again, his rage rising with every crash. Finally, he broke through. Within seconds he was inside. His gaze found Angus fiddling with the hooks of the window, while looking over his shoulder at the door. In a few strides, Rory reached the now open window and yanked Angus away from it.

Angus aimed a hit at him, and his fist connected with Rory's side. The pain fed his rising temper. He grabbed Angus by the shoulders, parried a kick aimed at his groin and pushed him into an armchair, almost toppling it over backwards. Wafts of brandy reached his nose. He grimaced in disgust. 'Twas only early afternoon and the man was already in his cups.

"What do you want, Cameron? I expected you to be dead by now." Angus' speech was slurred.

"Aye, I thought you might've wished for my head on a spike. But the judge thought differently." Rory sat opposite him, keeping a close eye on Angus and the door. The maid had disappeared, but Malcolm was now firmly installed at the open doorway. "Now, tell me where your sister is."

"Catriona? Why, she's visiting an aunt." Angus' gaze darted across the room.

"Your maid just said she's out riding."

"With her aunt." Defiance crept into Angus' voice. He sat with his legs and arms crossed. Defensive, sullen.

Rory chuckled sardonically. "Aye, and I have regular drinking sessions with the Green Man." He grew serious. "Where is she?"

"Like I said—"

Rory was upon him in an instant. Driving his knee into the sitting man's gut, he crouched over him, drew his dirk from his boot, and held it against Angus' neck. The young man's eyes widened, and his hands clawed Rory's face. "I'd sit still if I were you. My hand can get very shaky." A tiny trickle of blood showed stark against Angus' white skin, the red stark on his white neck kerchief.

"You bastard," Angus hissed but he dropped his hands, sitting still. Rory wrinkled his nose as the smell of alcohol nearly knocked him back.

Angus turned to Malcolm. "You're a soldier. Stop him!" But Malcolm simply turned his gaze to the papers in his hand.

Rory adjusted his grip on the knife. "Now, for the final time, where is your sister?"

In a whiny voice, Angus told him what he wanted to hear. "Catriona's been missing for two nights. The daft lass tried to escape, climbing down roped up sheets from her balcony."

Rory pushed himself off Angus. He turned away and took a deep breath. Admiration for Catriona's desperate action, warred with the fear inside him. They had little time to waste. Closing his mind of all the things Henderson might have done to her in the amount of time he had her, he focused on the list Malcolm handed him.

"The girl's clever, that's certain," Malcolm admitted and, looking over Rory's shoulder, turned to Angus who sat slumped in the armchair. "When did you last see Henderson?"

"First thing this morning. He said he had business to attend to. I was wondering if he'd taken her but I didn't dare ask," his voice faltered.

"Of course he's got her," Rory snarled at him, making Angus shrink even more into the padded leather. "And he'll pay for it." Casting another glance at the list, he discounted a couple of properties instantly. Henderson would not risk holding her where his father stayed, so that removed the city house and the country mansion from the list.

"What's this?" He pointed at a couple of addresses in a less salubrious area off High Street at the foot of the castle. The area with narrow lanes and filthy, cramped quarters. "St. Mary's Wynd, a workshop, and Pearson Close, an attic flat."

His mind raced. Both places were perfect for hiding someone from prying eyes. Not a soul would question a bundle being lugged about, and the noise and clamor would hide any screams.

"That's a good guess, Rory." Malcolm nodded.

"But which?" Rory wondered aloud.

"Pearson Close." A whisper escaped Angus' lips. "John talked about having some business to undertake in Pearson Close."

Rory shut his eyes for a second when Malcolm mused. "The narrowest lane in the city. Barely wide enough to allow two grown men to pass by one another, certainly not a place one would take notice."

"And it's an attic." Regaining his composure, Rory turned to Angus. "If anything happened to your sister, I'm holding you responsible."

The young man's face twisted into a sulky scowl. "Not my fault he got her." His gaze slid to the sideboard, where a crystal carafe held what looked like fine brandy. In two strides, Rory reached it, and hurled it into the fireplace. Shards of glass flew across the floor. Angus cowered in his seat as Rory stood over him. He hauled him upright and shook him so fiercely, his teeth clattered.

"Rory!" Malcolm's steadying hand on his shoulder stopped him from pummeling the obnoxious young man. He pushed Angus back into the chair. "I say it again, lad. If Catriona is hurt, you'll pay."

Rory turned on his heel and stalked from the room, Malcolm right behind him, pointing over his shoulder at the boy holding the reins of two horses at the bottom of the steps. The child grinned at them with crooked teeth, holding out the reins. Malcolm threw a couple of coins to the lad who caught them deftly, before he hurried down the lane.

Rory took a set of reins from Malcolm and jumped into the saddle. "I don't know how to thank you. Again."

Malcolm nodded. "You can thank me by rescuing the lass. I'll be off to the courts. I want to get the sergeants to look at Henderson's other places." He extended his hand, and Rory took it in a firm grip. "Who knows what they might find."

"Thank you, Malcolm. I couldn't have done this without you." With a final nod, Rory spurred his mount back toward High Street.

The buildings ahead of him rose high in the sky. He asked a peddler for Pearson Close and found it halfway up the hill. The view down the narrow lane was forbidding, the far end cloaked in darkness. Rory eased himself from the saddle and, leading his horse down the close, he saluted a wrinkled, bent shoemaker at a stall by a low window.

"Good day to you. Do you know of a flat down here belonging to one John Henderson? A dandy, tall, well-dressed?"

"Guess so, sir. Must be the one across there." The old man leaned out of his window and pointed a skinny finger at a flight of rickety, wooden stairs a little further down the lane. "A fine gentleman comes here sometimes to drop off...crates." He coughed surreptitiously. "Though this week 'twas a bundle."

Perhaps Malcolm should send the sergeants here, too. "Is it the top level?"

The man nodded, his few strands of hair falling over his wrinkled eyes. "Aye, the room just under the roof." His eyes lit, and Rory understood. The man suspected Henderson of dodgy affairs and wanted him caught.

"Thank you, sir. You may just have saved a life." Guessing the man too proud to accept any payment, he waved to the young apprentice hovering in the background. "Can you take care of my horse while I go up? It'll be worth your while."

The youth grinned broadly, doffing his cap. He jumped over the window ledge and took the reins. "Aye, sir. Don't ye worry. He's safe wi' me." The old man's eyes twinkled as he returned to his workbench.

Rory strode down the lane, dodging a mangy dog sniffing at something he'd rather not explore closer. The stench oozing from the cobbled ground was nauseating. He squeezed past a stall selling pots and looked at the stairs pointed out by the shoemaker. With a determined jump, he took the steps two at a time. He was halfway up when he looked to the top of the close. John Henderson's lanky form stood upright, framed by bright daylight. Their eyes met. Rory held his breath. Henderson turned his head as if to check behind him that the path was clear. Sending a final glance toward Rory, he backed out of the lane.

Rory swore. Every fiber of his being itched to run after the man, to punish him for taking Catriona but he shook it off. *Let him go!* Malcolm's men will find him. At the top step he paused outside a wooden door with a sturdy lock. Looking down, the height made him dizzy.

"Steady!" Rory held on to the flimsy wooden plank that served as a banister and focused his gaze on the door. There was little space for much leverage against the solid wood, and if he lost his balance, he knew where he'd be headed.

Stepping back as far as he dared, he took a deep breath and hit the lock with his boot. The metal shook but held. Another couple of kicks made it rattle, but still the door did not budge. A scream coming from inside froze his heart. His pulse raced as he rattled at the lock.

"Catriona," he shouted through the barrier separating them. A movement further down the stairs made him turn. The shoemaker's apprentice came pounding up the stairs. "Sir!"

Sharing the little space they had, the apprentice grinned at him, brandishing a set of what looked like sharp hooks. "We're not just mendin' shoes, sir." He turned to the door and tried a few sets, twisting them back and forth in the lock. Finally, they heard a loud click.

"Thank you, lad."

The boy stepped back. Turning the handle, Rory shoved the door open.

His heart froze. A dark bundle lay on the floor in the middle of the room. His eyes slowly adjusted to the dim light, and he heard her whimper.

"Cat," he whispered and rushed to her side. She kept her eyes closed and struggled when he tried to lift her into his arms.

"No! Leave me be." Her voice barely audible, she drove her shoulder into his side, all the while struggling to be free.

"Catriona," he said louder. "It's me, Rory. Shhh." Her eyes flew open, blinking against the daylight streaming through the open door. As recognition dawned, he gathered her into his arms and rocked her gently as she cried.

"Rory! You're alive."

"Hush now, my love. I'll get you out of here." He turned to see the apprentice hovering in the doorframe. "Can you get my horse to the bottom of the stairs, lad?"

"Aye, sir." The boy disappeared from sight, loud steps pounding down the steps.

"Now here," Rory murmured. "Let's see to this." He pulled his dirk from his boot and cut loose her hands. Catriona sat back, rubbing her chafed wrists. The blade sliced through the cords at her feet and with a sigh, she stretched her leg. He took her hands and massaged her wrists. Her eyes large, they held his gaze for what seemed like an eternity.

"I'm so sorry." He swallowed hard. It tore his heart out seeing her in this state. Her arms were raw, and a purple bruise covered her elbow. She shook like a leaf. He drew her into his arms and rested her head on his shoulder. Only then did he smell the blood, felt the stickiness on her hair.

Rory withdrew a few inches, his hand exploring the wound above her temple. She flinched but held still.

"Sorry, lass. This needs mending. Can you stand?" She nodded, and he pulled her up with him. As her legs gave way, he scooped her into his arms. Her lips were tantalizingly close to his and need proved too strong. Pulling her closer still, his mouth brushed hers. A shudder went through him. Nothing had ever felt so right.

Slowly, he lifted his head. "Hold on tight, Cat. We have a steep climb down ahead of us." A wave of emotions raked through him when she draped her arms tight around his neck, resting her head on his shoulder.

He'd take care of her.

Chapter Nineteen

Catriona woke to the sound of birdsong drifting through the open window. Sunlight beamed around the edges of the curtains swaying in the morning breeze, bathing the room in a golden glow. No noisy crowds, no carts rushing up and down the streets. Simple, pure bliss.

A knock on her door pulled her from her dreams. "Come in." She sat up, pulling the covers to cover her chest. Mairi entered, bearing a tray of porridge and tea, and set it on the bed.

"There you go, lass. You'll be in fine fettle in no time."

Catriona laughed as she balanced the tray on her knees. "Mairi, I've been back a full week and might end up as fat as a goose if I keep eating at this rate. I'm fine now. Honestly," she added, seeing the look of worry on the girl's face. Mairi was so much more than a maid. She was like the sister Catriona never had.

"You can never be certain. Will you go riding again today? Rory doesn't like it when you go off on your own, and he's gone out for the morning."

Catriona shrugged. "Well, I can't wait for him all day. Yes, I'd like to go for a ride after breaking my fast. I don't want to waste such a beautiful day."

"It certainly is that," Mairi said, pulling the curtains open. Catriona squinted in the glare of the morning sun.

"I can't be stuck indoors just because Rory worries. He always worries." Blowing on a spoonful of steaming porridge to cool it, she blushed. It seemed like the whole community suspected something was afoot between Rory and her, even though he'd kept his distance the last few days. Catriona guessed it was due to her ongoing recovery. "Where did he go?"

Mairi shrugged. "Rory goes where he has to go. This time I think it's something to do with that horrible man, Henderson. He's still on the run, and I know Major Campbell's keen to catch him."

Catriona shivered and put the spoon down. "I wish they would. Actually, I wish he were dead. That way he'd never threaten another woman again." She put the tray to the side, her appetite lost.

The maid went to the clothes peg, picking up Catriona's simple, grey riding gown and jacket. "They'll catch him, no worries. Henderson's not liked anywhere in the Highlands so wherever he's hiding, someone will betray him. Sooner or later. Even Jamie's joined the hunt, although he keeps at a wise distance from the Redcoats. He's speaking to folk around Stirling where Henderson was last spotted. Sometimes folk rather speak to one of their own than a Redcoat. He's already provided Major Campbell with important information."

The sound of pride in Mairi's voice made Catriona's smile. The pair had become inseparable. No doubt, Jamie would find the courage soon to speak to Rory about their plans.

"Yes, he's doing very well, Rory told me. My brother hasn't seen John either. He said so in the letter I received yesterday. In fact, Angus sounded quite subdued." Catriona pushed the covers away and went to the washbasin, to dip her hands in the cool water. She splashed her face, and then dried it with a linen towel. "I think the debt collectors are back at his door and nobody's around to help him. This time he'll have to sort out his own mess." Satisfied with her brother's troubles, she slid out of her night clothes and held up her arms for Mairi to help her dress.

***

The breeze played with loose strands of her hair as she rode at a canter up the lochside path. Warmed by the sun, she watched as seagulls landed on the glistening water, the gentle waves mirroring deep blue against the cloudless sky. The atmosphere was peaceful, the landscape covered with colorful little dots, heathers and wildflowers swaying in the breeze. It was paradise.

Realization hit her just as she approached the boathouse. Yes, this was her home now for the rest of her life. At least she hoped. Rory had not yet asked for her hand, nor had he uttered those little three little words she was so desperate to hear. Every time they were together he was attentive, charming, holding her hand, touching her neck, and stroking her face. Yet, he always refrained from kissing her and slid away from any embrace she sought. Perhaps she was wrong, and he did not love her after all. Perhaps he just agreed to her being here, to share his home because he felt sorry for her? Tears welled up, and she stifled a sob.

Catriona brought her mount to a halt outside the boathouse. Did Rory ever return to the cave? This was most dangerous, with the military boats now patrolling the loch both day and night.

She tied the reins to a branch and went to the door. The rusty hinges creaked when she pulled it open, and she stood still, her eyes adjusting to the dimness inside. She saw the boat, tied to a stake, swaying against the floorboards. Relief flooded her, and she balled her hands into fists to keep them from shaking. Rory had not ventured out on the water. Perhaps he was already back at the house looking for her? She should return.

As Catriona turned away from the darkness, a movement to her side caught her by surprise. Her hand on the latch, she gasped when someone pulled her by the hair from behind. Rough hands shoved her to the floor on her belly, taking her breath away. She tried to push herself off the ground but a knee in the small of her back held her in place. The dirk hidden in the folds of her dress was out of reach.

"Good morning, Catriona. It's so good to see you up and about."

"John!" Her body shuddered, and she closed her eyes

momentarily. Rory and Mairi were right. She'd been foolish to go out alone. "What are you doing here?"

His hand at the base of her neck made her skin crawl. "We have unfinished business. I'm here for payment. This time I'm going to make sure I get it." He lifted his weight off her and flipped her over. Catriona kicked out with her legs but her riding dress, with the petticoats underneath, hampered her. John hit her with his fist. She wheezed, clawing at her cheek.

He pushed up her skirts, one hand pressing onto her middle to pin her down.

Catriona screamed, her vision spinning from the impact, and blood pounded in her ears.

"Oh yes, lie back, dear. You'll enjoy it just as much as I will." He ripped her skirts apart and, fending off her kicking legs, squeezed himself between them. His hand raked up her thighs, nails scratching her skin.

She hissed in pain as his fingers dug into her flesh. "Stop," she whispered, her voice hoarse with pain.

She lashed out at him but regretted it the same moment when his fist came crashing into her stomach. The punch knocked the wind from her. Refusing to let him see her tears and her pain, Catriona closed her eyes, pretending to faint.

"Oh no, Catriona! I won't let you go. I'm not finished with you yet." His voice shuddering with excitement, John began to loosen his breeches.

"I think you are, Henderson. Finished, that is. Make one more move and you'll be dead. Please, give me an excuse."

"Rory!" Catriona opened her eyes to see Rory pointing a pistol at John's head. John turned sharply, his hand aiming to knock the pistol from Rory's grasp but this time Rory was prepared, moving just out of reach.

"Let her go," Rory growled, and the unleashed fury in his gaze made Catriona shiver. He made a dangerous enemy.

John turned to her, a wolfish grin on his face. He forced her up and ducked behind her, the sharp blade of a dirk at her throat. "Look who's got the upper hand now, Cameron. You don't want anything to happen to your little darling, do you?"

He pulled Catriona up and dragged her with him toward the boat. When she tried to twist from his grasp, a searing pain stung her. He'd nicked her neck. A slow trickle of blood dripped down her dress. Her eyes met Rory's, reading the cold determination in them.

Rory would find a way. She trusted him.

Untying the rope holding the boat, John stepped into it, always holding her in front of him. The small vessel rocked on the soft waves as he tried to keep the balance. Rory could not get a clear shot unless she moved but John did not give her a chance. He sat on a plank, dragging her down with him.

"Take the oars and push us off," he hissed into her ear, the blade scratching her throat. Catriona reached for the oars and pushed the boat off the walkway, letting it float out into open water. Panic welled in her chest. What if John made her row to the other side of the loch? Rory could never get across in time.

"Faster!" A slap on the back of her head made her tumble, but he jerked her right back. "Not so fast, dearie."

Oh, how she hated the patronizing sound of his voice. Turning, Catriona saw him watching her, eyes squinting against the bright sunlight. She looked back at the shore, watching Rory stand by the water's edge, pistol aimed at them. Her chances were draining away. Once out of reach, she was entirely at John's mercy.

Sensing John peeking over her shoulder at the shore, she rammed an elbow into his face. A crunching sound told her she'd broken his nose. He fell backwards with a scream, the dirk flying into the water.

Catriona scrambled out of his reach causing the boat to tilt. Arms flailing in the air, she barely kept her balance. The oars went overboard as the rocking grew more violent. Blood spurted from John's nose. His gaze, full of hatred, never left her. When he rose, she moved further away from him, but the hem of her gown caught on a rusty nail. John inched toward her. Eyes bulging, he snarled at her as he stretched out a hand to grab her dress. Catriona kicked her feet, and he straightened again.

A shot rang out across the water, echoing off the hills around them. John's gaze turn dull, as blood gushed from a scarlet hole in his forehead. Another shot hit him in the chest, sending him backwards into the water. Gripping the edge of the boat, she stared after him as his body sank into the depths. Was he really gone? Unable to wrench her gaze from the spot where he vanished, her body began to shiver.

A shout drifted through her daze.

Rory!

With her hands clinging to the planks, Catriona turned and watched him throw his pistol and a musket to the ground, remove his shirt, and tug off his boots. In two strides he was in the water, swimming steadily toward the boat. Terrified John might hide under the surface and attack him, Catriona peeked over the edge, but his body had disappeared without a trace.

Moments later, Rory reached the boat, having collected the loose oars. She took them, and the boat rocked when he heaved himself in. The look in his eyes, full of fear and love, told her all she needed to know. He balanced the boat with his knees and drew her close. Cradling her in his arms, he whispered to her soothing words in Gaelic, his breath hot on her chilled skin, until her breathing calmed.

Catriona nestled her head against his chest, her ear against his heart, and her heartbeat slowed in unison with his.

"He's gone," he croaked in English, his voice ragged. "He's gone." He held her at a hand's breadth, raking his gaze over her before slowly releasing her. "Let's go home."

She leaned back against the wood, reaching for his hand and holding it tight. Rory was here. All was good.

***

As Rory sat by her bedside later that night, he looked her over, concern mingling with the anger still boiling within him. The scrapes at her neck and face were a faint hue of purple, and the cut at her throat, sure to turn into a scar, a constant reminder. He swore.

Never again.

"You're mine now," he whispered. His heart skipped a beat as a smile spread across her peaceful face, lost in sleep. He leaned back, contentment slowly overcoming his rage. Henderson was dead. Angus was in disgrace. And Catriona was all his.

A sense of guilt mingled with the love bursting from his heart as he sat, watching her.

The hour was late when Rory returned to his chamber. He had sat by Catriona's bedside for most of the night, and had come to a decision, having spent the hours in serious thought.

Uncaring, he dropped his clothes on the floor by the bed. Tiredness washed over him as he blew out the candle. The itching of the scars on his back more irritating than painful now, he leaned into the soft pillows. At last, he closed his eyes and exhaled on a sigh.

A hesitant knock on the door made him open them again. The door slid open, and he watched as a slim, female form sneaked in and locked it behind her. Rory smiled when Catriona stepped tentatively across the dim room, slivers of moonlight guiding her way. The gleam illuminated soft curves underneath her thin shift. He licked his suddenly dry lips.

"Catriona," he whispered, his voice hoarse. Heat shot through him. He threw the covers back and stretched out his hand for her. "Are you well?"

"I didn't want to be alone." She put her hand in his, her eyes wide. Her gaze traveled along his body, his need for her plain to see. She stopped short by his side, as if unsure what to do next.

Rory kneeled on the bed in front of her, stroking her face. "You're not alone, Catriona. Never again will you be alone. Never again will I fail you."

Soft fingers touched his cheek. "You didn't fail me, Rory. You saved me."

When she spoke, she tilted her head to see his face and now was so close her breath kissed his lips. He could not seem to stop touching her. "I want you to love me," Catriona said. "I want you to make me yours."

"Are you sure?" he asked. "After all you've suffered? You still need rest and may recon—"

"Sshhh." Her fingers brushed over his lips. "I'm certain, Rory. You can help me forget. Make love to me."

She smiled, a shy smile that started a fire raging within him. His hands slid down her neck, along the rim of her shift. She shivered under his touch. In one smooth move, he pulled the shift over her head, exposing her to him. How long had he waited for this moment!

Rory's breath faltered. "You are beautiful." Pulling her toward him, hands gliding down her back, his lips explored the slender line of her neck, nibbled the soft spot under her earlobe. A soft moan escaped her lips, and she leaned closer, her hands roaming his chest with the lightest of touches.

"Come to me," he said as he pulled her down with him, cradling her head in the crook of his arm. He sealed her lips with a searing kiss.

Epilogue

Catriona's hand shook as she tried to keep the candle steady, scattering droplets of wax onto the stone floor. Rory crouched next to her, releasing the sliding rock to reveal the entrance to the cave with the shimmering ceiling. It was his idea to come here, following the trail of the mysterious seal which she insisted saved her from the soldiers.

"Have you ever seen any seals here?" she asked. Taking his offered hand, she slid in behind him before he pulled the trigger to seal the entrance.

Rory shook his head. "No, but I've heard them often enough." Seeing the surprise in her eyes, he laughed. "Dozens of seals come to the loch each year. It's perfectly possible one or two found this cave for shelter."

"Ahh," she whispered as she held the candle aloft, bringing the ceiling to sparkle. Hues of green and blue, red and yellow, vied for supremacy in the shimmering light.

They rounded several stalagmites and found a flat spot, with a straight wall behind them. Rory pulled a blanket from his bag and, shaking it out, laid it onto the ground. A couple of cushions followed.

"It's not much, but it'll do. Please sit, Cat."

The solemn sound of his voice made her search his face. Fear gripped her heart for a moment, but the love in his eyes soothed her. She sat and leaned against the wall, adjusting her skirts as she stretched her legs in front of her.

He knelt next to her and took her hand. Linking her fingers in his, he smiled, brushing a loose strand of hair from her eyes with the other hand.

"I've brought you here as this is a special place. A magical place. And I want only one person in the world to share the magic." He held his hand up when she wanted to respond. "Hear me out. Because first of all I owe you an apology."

"An apology?"

"Aye. I misjudged you. When you first arrived at *Taigh na Rhon* I worried you might drive a wedge between Auntie Meg and me. I feared you might take my place in her affections."

"But—"

"Shh, *mo chridhe*. But it wasn't just that, I also took you for a...a..." Words failed him.

"Strumpet," she helped, smiling. "I know what you thought of me. And I can't blame you. Angus left everyone in little doubt."

Rory shook his head. "I don't deserve your understanding, Cat. I was wrong." His voice broke and he looked at the ceiling, his eyes filled with tears. "I never wanted you to get hurt. That's why I...I pushed you away. To keep you safe. Little did I know—"

"Rory," Catriona whispered. Her hand reached out and pulled him toward her. Guilt plagued his dear features. "It's nothing to worry about. You came to help me, and nearly lost your life. And then you saved me. I forgive you if that's what you seek."

He nodded. "You're not angry with me?"

"No." She firmly shook her head, patting the space next to her. "Come, sit beside me. Enjoy the wonder of the cave. I've seen too much grief lately. This is healing time."

Rory lowered himself and settled her into the crook of his arm. Catriona lay her head back and let her gaze roam over the flickering colors of the ceiling. Finally, she was at peace.

"I love you, Rory." The words escaped her lips. Heat rose in her cheeks, and she closed her eyes, afraid she might have pushed him away.

But then something cold slid over the third finger of her left hand. She lifted it and stared at a solid gold ring, a large ruby set in its center. Its sparkle rivaled the cave's ceiling.

"What's this?" Catriona held her breath as Rory turned to

her.

"It's Auntie Meg's wedding band," he whispered, mouth trembling inches from hers, eyes large with hope. "Wed me, Cat. Be my bride."

Her heart raced. A sweet dizziness threatened her, but she beamed at him. Tears stung her eyes, and her heart fluttered. "I'll gladly wed you, Rory Cameron. Gladly."

With shaky hands Rory encircled her face, his fingers like feathers on her skin. "I love you. Mo *chridhe,* my heart." He sighed, trailing light kisses over her face. She shivered at the delicious sensation.

With a sigh of delight, she met his hungry mouth. For once in her life, she was happy. This was where she belonged.

With Rory.

As they lay entwined on the blanket, leaning into the soft cushions, Catriona was certain she heard the seal bark before a splash burst through the silence. She held her breath as the sound of water lapping slowly receded.

Rory chuckled and pulled her even closer. "See, the legend is real."

"Yes, it is." Catriona smiled back at him before her gaze drifted to his curved mouth.

Just one more kiss.

THE END

Author's Note

Highland Arms started off as a *NaNoWriMo* (National Novel Writing Month) project. I didn't finish it in time, but embellished and completed it over the course of the next half year. The location, on the shores of Loch Linnhe, with the dramatic backdrop of Glencoe, is my favorite place in Scotland and an area we have visited many times. It is most inspiring!

Whilst the novel was always going to be about a romance between a Lowland girl and a rebellious Highlander, the idea of introducing smuggling was borne out of several booklets I found on sale in the Ballachulish Tourist Centre. They gave me an invaluable insight into local customs and culture, and I'm very grateful to their author, Barbara Fairweather. The Glencoe Folk Museum is also worth a visit as it gives you a wonderful glimpse of life in the past.

The scene in Edinburgh where Catriona is locked up was inspired by a visit (the first of many) to The Real Mary King's Close (**www.realmarykingsclose.com**). The tour takes you to the forgotten streets of Edinburgh, now located below the Royal Mile. Pearson Close did indeed exist, with its multi-storey tenements, and its history is worth exploring.

Thank you for reading this Ocelot Press book.

If you enjoyed it, we would greatly
appreciate it if you could take a moment
to write a short review.

You might also like to try books by fellow
Ocelot Press authors. We cover a small range of
genres, with a focus on historical fiction (including
mystery and paranormal), romance and fantasy.

Find Ocelot Press at:
Website: **www.ocelotpress.wordpress.com**
Facebook: **www.facebook.com/OcelotPress**
Twitter: **www.twitter.com/OcelotPress**

Printed in Great Britain
by Amazon